THE
TRUTH
ABOUT
GRACE

A sequel to The Pecan Man

Cassie Dandridge Selleck

Published by Obstinate Daughters Press, Lady Lake, Florida 2018
Edited by Patricia C. Walker of Obstinate Daughters Press

Other works by Cassie Dandridge Selleck

The Pecan Man

What Matters in Mayhew
Volume One of the Beanie Bradsher Series

Dedication

*In memory of Laurie Dawn "Petey" Dandridge
and Jamey Lea Jones.*

*This novel is dedicated to families struggling with
the heartbreak of addiction and to the professionals
who help them.*

Acknowledgements

Thanks to my own Obstinate Daughters Patti Walker, Katie Emily and Emily Selleck. You keep me sane, grounded, motivated, and laughing at every turn. I am proud of the strong, beautiful, obstinate women you have become.

Special thanks to Patti Walker, Senior Editor of Obstinate Daughters Press, and my own personal editor. Her incredible editing skills and keen awareness of character and plot have made crucial differences in the story, and I am profoundly grateful.

A huge shout out to my writers group, Gainesville Poets and Writers, who have been meeting every Tuesday night for over thirty years and whose input keeps me plugging away.

Special thanks to Jani Sherard and Fern Musselwhite for your thoughtful insight and encouragement, and for going the extra mile to be my beta readers. You were both tremendous help to me.

To my besties Teresa Renfrow Masters and Julie Williams Sanon, thanks for loving me exactly as I am and being my biggest cheerleaders. I love you so much!

And to my husband Perry, thanks for your patience, support and endless contributions to our home. Most of all, thanks for "coffee with love" in the mornings. You are my heart.

Prologue

Ora Lee Beckworth

In the summer of 1976, I hired a homeless black man to mow my lawn and tend my gardens, such as they were. My neighbors were none too happy with my choice of employees. He carried pecans he'd collected in a bag hung from the handlebars of the rickety old bicycle he rode. They called him the Pecan Man and thought he had an air of something sinister. I just thought he looked hungry and offered him a job. His name was Eldred Mims. I called him Eddie. Blanche, my housekeeper at the time and employee for many years afterwards, warned me about sticking my nose where it didn't belong. I took that as a challenge and pressed on.

I'd been widowed less than a year, but Blanche had been raising five children on the salary I paid her, plus Social Security benefits, since her husband died in 1970. Her oldest, Marcus, was in the Army at Fort Bragg. Patrice was a senior in high school with a promising future. Her twins Re'Netta and Danita were twelve and Grace, the youngest, was only six.

In early fall, Grace, a beautiful child with the sweetest nature I had ever known, was raped by Skipper Kornegay, the son of the local police chief. I was stunned when Blanche, fearing repercussions from townspeople and mistreatment of her child, refused to report the assault.

I had lived through the civil rights protests in the South and was opposed to Jim Crow laws and segregation, though I can't say I was active in the movement. I certainly disapproved of the mistreatment of other human beings; it went against everything my Methodist upbringing taught me about Jesus Christ. But Walter, my husband, had a business to run, and it was never a good idea to discuss religion or politics, so I stayed out of it.

If it had been the 1950's or even the 60's, I might have understood Blanche's concern, but this was 1976. The times were changing, I thought. Surely Blanche could trust that her child would be treated fairly and receive justice for such a brutal crime. It took some time and a change of perspective to make me realize how wrong I was.

At the time, though – despite my misgivings – I went along with her decision. It was simply not mine to make. At least that's how I consoled myself back then. We told no one about the rape, not even her own children. We did our best to control a tidal wave of lies that began with this: *It was just a dream.* But everyone knows control is an illusion.

Eldred Mims was the one who'd found Gracie bleeding and crying in the woods and brought her home to us, but he disappeared shortly afterwards, and we did not see him again for several weeks. When he returned, we invited him to have Thanksgiving dinner with us. It was the first time Blanche's family shared the meal with me and I was looking forward to the company. Afterwards Eddie, not knowing we'd kept it a secret, let it slip to Marcus that his baby sister had been assaulted. Later that evening, Marcus ran into Skipper coming out of a local pool hall. The details are too many to describe here, but when it was over, Skipper lay dead in the woods, stabbed multiple times with his own knife.

For reasons only he knew at the time, Eddie confessed to Skipper's murder. Now, twenty-five years later, Eddie has died in prison, and I knew he was innocent all along. Days before Eddie's funeral, wanting to clear my conscience and Eddie's name, I dictated a confession of sorts to my dear friend Clara Jean Smallwood. She worked as the personal secretary to the Honorable Harley Odell for as long as I can remember and up until he retired just before the turn of the millennium. Harley and I had been friends since elementary school – long enough for me to call him by his childhood name, Poopsie, and long before we were integrated in the South. Of course, just because Clara was a legal assistant doesn't mean the confession was anything official. I just wanted to get the story told so the families affected by my actions could finally know the truth.

I don't know what's going to happen to me and, quite frankly, I'm not sure I care. I've been alone for so many years now, I've grown weary of my own self. Truth be told, I was alone most of my life, despite a great deal of civic and social interaction. It's why I kept Blanche working full-time up until the day she died. I didn't need a housekeeper, or a personal assistant as she came to be. I just found things for her to do because I liked having her around. Besides Poopsie, she was probably the only real friend I ever had. I think I expected she would end up caring for me in my old age. But here I am now, outliving them all.

I don't want to be alone anymore. I've been having spells that scare me half to death. I'm afraid I'll fall down the stairs and lay there for days in my own waste before anyone finds me, dead or alive. I'm starting to understand how Eddie could have found prison a relief, though I wish to everything holy that life had given him better options. I wish *I* had given him better options. But I didn't. I let him carry a burden that belonged to people who ought to know better, myself included.

There were so many lies told, so many mistakes made, and the one who got the worst of it all was Gracie. In trying to protect her – as we believed in our hearts we were doing – we pushed her aside, and the consequences have been devastating. I told all the story I knew to tell. It's time for others to speak. It's time we learned the truth about Grace.

Part 1 – March 2001

1 – Grace

What the hell does she want from me? That's what I wanna know. Am I supposed to throw my arms around her neck and shout hallelujah?

I gotta stop thinkin' about all this. It's exhausting. Here I am, the mornin' after we buried Mr. Pecan, alone in a white woman's kitchen. Kinda feels like home somehow, or at least familiar. I put on a pot of coffee and sat back down at the table to rest my eyes.

I was still sitting there, my head on my arms, when I heard her tiptoeing down the stairs. Her house so old, all the floors creak no matter how soft you step. Miss Ora don't weigh a minute; she tiny and shriveled up even more than I remember.

"I smell coffee," she said.

Her kitchen ain't changed much over the years. The cabinets are still the same – solid wood doors painted white. But I can reach the ones above the counter now. Those thin china plates with the silver and white flowers are no longer off limits to my wandering hands. I made jelly toast this mornin' and used what Mama called Miss Ora's "good china." There was a part of me wanted to drop it into her porcelain sink, just to see it shatter. I could have lied and said it was an accident. Wouldn't be the first lie told in this kitchen. After I washed and dried that little plate, I traced my fingers over the tiny flowers, felt their thin outlines rise up off the plate. I looked closer at it then and saw my own face staring back at me. My eyes were wide like I was surprised to see myself. I hugged the plate to my chest and put it back in the cabinet where it belonged. Decided I didn't need Sister griping about me messin' with Miss Ora's things.

She and Aunt Tressa are coming back sometime this morning. They told me last night before they left. I don't remember everything that happened last night, but I know one thing. I don't ever want to feel that way again – like the room is closing in on me – like all I gotta do is let go and it'll swallow me up. There been times I didn't wanna live no more – even thought about killin' myself – but I'm scared I'd mess that up too.

I lifted my head from my arms and studied her. Then the memory just about knocked me over. Me sittin' here in her kitchen the day after I was raped. This right here is where my whole life shattered. Not out there in the woods behind town where that white boy raped me, though that didn't help none. No, it was right here where my mama broke me. Just a dream, my ass. I was a baby, barely six years old. I remember wakin' up and wobblin' into the kitchen. It was the first time I'd ever spent the night at Miss Ora's house. Mama was there cooking breakfast, so I sat down at the table and fell back asleep until Miss Ora came down and woke me up. I was sore all over, including in a place I ain't never felt pain before.

Sittin' here now, the pain was so real I almost flinched.

"Are you all right, Gracie?"

I took the cup she offered me. Her hands were shaking.

"Fine, thanks," I said, but I didn't really mean it and she could tell.

"You stayed the night," she said. She has a habit of sayin' what's obvious.

"Patrice made me. I didn't want to." I wiped at my eyes with both hands. I'd cried so much the night before, they were dry and crusty and itched like hell.

"I'm glad you did. I rarely have the pleasure of company in the morning. I was so used to Blanche being here..." She caught herself then. I could tell she was embarrassed. "I miss her."

I nodded. I miss her too, but I wasn't in the mood for bein' sentimental.

She raised her cup under her nose and said, "Smells just like your mama's."

"Huh," I said. "Not like the kind she made at home. Smells like *your* coffee to me."

"Grace..."

She sat down in the chair beside me. Her cup rattled on the saucer.

"Grace," she began again, "I want you to know that I'm sorry for what happened. No, let me say that differently. I'm sorry for what I did. I'm sorry you were hurt by it. I'm sorry we let you down. I want to tell you the whole story, but I'm also very torn by what I believe is an obligation to your mama..."

"My mama is dead." I sat straight up in my chair and pointed my finger first at her, then at myself. "You don't owe the dead, Miss Ora. The way I see it, you owe the livin', and that's me."

"Fair enough," she said. "What do you want to know?"

Every time I think I have my head wrapped around the truth, I find something else to twist back in shape. "Why'd y'all lie to me? That's

6

the first thing. I tried to ask Patrice about it last night, but she swears she didn't know."

"She did *not* know."

"Because if she did, then even her taking my children when Mama died takes on a whole new meaning." Patrice has been mad at me for so long, it just feels like part of who she is. Who *we* are. I always felt like I was raised by two mothers, and I disappointed 'em both.

Miss Ora shook her head back and forth a long time. "She absolutely *did not* know. We told no one."

"That judge asked me about it, too. Did he know?" I asked.

"Poopsie?"

"Say what?"

"Judge Odell. Poopsie is what I called him."

"Yeah, Odell. You know he paid for me to go to rehab one time?"

She nodded. "I did know. I had a trust fund set up for you and he was the overseer. I rescinded it when we lost track of you for so long."

I had to sit with that one for a minute to figure out what it meant. This is what I'm talkin' about – I have to rethink every truth I thought I knew. Can't rely on a damn thing.

"You mean you the one paid for my rehab?"

She nodded.

"And all this time I thought he was just a nice man."

"He *was* a nice man," she said. "He was a good friend of mine, and he had suspicions, but he never knew what happened to you."

"Was? He dead, too?"

"He is," Miss Ora stood and picked up her coffee cup. "A lot of people had to die before I could tell this story."

She walked into the kitchen and slid her cup and saucer into the sink. Then she turned around and faced me.

"And the truth is, I could go to jail for telling it, so don't just assume I'm doing this for myself. For my conscience? Maybe. But more likely for my eternal soul. It's certainly not a convenient story to tell." She came back to the table and sat down beside me. "Grace, honey, we can't go back, but *we can* go forward. I'll do anything I can to help you get well, as long as you are *trying* to get well."

"I ain't tryin' to be sick, that's for sure."

"Are you staying at your mom's house still?" she asked.

"Yeah, Patrice had it fixed up for me."

"Could you do something for me? I mean, could you consider doing something?"

This woman takes the cake, I'm just sayin'. I swigged the last bit of cold coffee from my cup.

"What is it?"

"Could you stay here a while? I mean *stay* here. Could you move in here for just a couple of weeks until we see what happens?"

"I don't need to be babysat, Miss Ora. I ain't using."

"I didn't say you were." She stopped and wrung her hands like she was putting on lotion. "I just... I mean, for once in my life I don't want to be alone. I don't know what's going to happen to me, and I know that sounds selfish, and way too much to put on you, but still...would you?"

I was still shaking my head over this when I went back to my room. I'm still mad, too. But, I spent a lot of time at this house when I was a girl. It was Miss Ora got me hooked on reading. My very first addiction, I guess you could call it. That ain't even funny, but there it is.

I guess I'll get Patrice to take me back to Mama's house this afternoon so I can pack my bags. Looks like I'll be moving in with an old white woman for a while.

2 – Patrice

I left my sister at Miss Ora's house last night. It was against my better judgment, but my opinion was ignored, as usual. Aunt Tressa is going to meet me there later this morning. Feels odd to call someone you barely know something so personal. Aunt Tressa. That's how Miss Ora introduced us yesterday at Eddie's funeral. "Girls, I want you to meet your Aunt Tressa. She was your mother's sister."

Now, as far as we knew, my mother never had a sister, or a brother, either. For that matter, she had no father. Hers left right after she was born. But, with that one introduction, an entire family was revealed to us. Just like that. Sometimes I wonder what Miss Ora could possibly be thinking. With all that Southern upbringing, didn't anyone ever teach her the art of subtlety? Apparently not.

It's hard to complain about her, though. She's the reason I'm an attorney now. Obviously, I did the work, but she made it possible and, despite what feels like an enormous betrayal right now, I owe her a lot.

I wanted to crawl back in bed this morning and just pretend like none of this happened. Shawn and Rochelle put that notion straight out of my head. There were lunches to pack, homework to sign. I went from being a single career woman to a surrogate mother the day my mother had a stroke and never woke up again. She was, for all practical purposes, the only mother they ever knew, but they were not hers either. I have been raising my sister's children for the past three years.

They were full of questions this morning. So much for pretending.

"Who was Eddie again?" Rochelle asked at breakfast. She is tall and wiry for a twelve-year-old. I plan on pushing her toward law school in the future. I've heard you can tell what a child's purpose in life is by how she is as a child. Rochelle is all elbows and knees and endless interrogation.

"Eddie was Gramma's father," I explained patiently – for the third time. "That would make him your grandfather."

"Is that what we called him? Grandfather?" Rochelle wiped butter off her cheek with the back of her hand.

"We didn't call him anything, Ro, don't be stupid." Shawn stood, grabbing his ball cap from the table and towering over his sister. "We never met him before."

"Hey now," I said. "Play fair. You haven't always been the same model of brilliance you are today."

He grinned at me then. He is easily annoyed, but just as easily teased into his true nature, which is friendly and easygoing.

"If we never met him before, how come we went to his funeral yesterday?" Rochelle persisted.

"Because he died. Duh." Shawn smacked his sister on the back of the head, grabbed his lunch bag and headed for the door. "I'll be in the car."

"Uh, garbage?" I shouted at his retreating back.

"Took it out last night!" he hollered just before I heard the car door slam.

"Come on, Ro, let's get this show on the road," I said. "Go brush your teeth and, for crying out loud, do something with your hair or I'm gonna take you over to Aunt Re'Netta's shop and make her cut it."

Rochelle whined something back at me, but I didn't hear what it was. We have a nice comfortable relationship, these kids and I. Somebody's always rocking the boat, but someone's always there to settle it down, too.

I'd like to think this news will be a catalyst for Grace. She has been through so much, and she has put the family through hell. But this news creates a paradigm shift the likes of which none of us have seen. All I can do is brace myself. I have a feeling there is a huge storm coming.

3 – Grace

I've got to hand it to Miss Ora – she knows how to make a room comfortable. I was so tired last night, I probably didn't need the sleeping pill Aunt Tressa gave me. I took it though, and I slept good in this soft old bed. We stayed up awful late, my sisters and I, talking about... well... everything. It's a lot. A lot to take in. First off, my Aunt Tressa. I could have told you she was my aunt the second I met her, which was only yesterday. She looks like a cross between Patrice and Mama, which is hard to look at, I ain't lyin'. She's tall and straight-boned like Patrice, more angles than curves, with skin smooth as caramel icing. But her face is like Mama's; her eyes are pale gold wishing for green, and only the top half of her lids show when her eyes are open. Mama's face was always hard-set, but it was so round and soft that it was hard to take her serious. She was a good liar though, I'll give her that.

I'm not stupid. I mean, I knew what happened to me. No way an innocent child could dream somethin' she ain't never seen. I knew what that white-headed boy did to me, but my mama tol' me so many times, I think it actually *became* a dream. A haunting that crept inside my skin and crawled out at night like tiny cockroaches. Especially when I was cranked up. I dug at those ghost bugs until I left scars all over my body. One time, I was so sure there was a spider tryin' to come out from under my chin that I took a pair of scissors and cut a chunk out of my neck. Ended up in the hospital that time, and my first trip to rehab. Mama was still alive then. I hate she had to see that, but I can't take all the blame. Would I be here if they'd told me the truth to begin with? I don't think so.

I ain't ever got over that boy hurtin' me like he did. That laugh...oh, God, that laugh. The bugs laughed just like him.

And where did I go all these years tryin' to escape those little phantoms? To the library. I went to books. Sounds crazy, doesn't it? But that's what I did. It was the only thing that eased my mind, especially when I was coming down. I would find a big armchair tucked away in a corner and read books by people who looked like me. Much as I loved Jane Eyre in high school, I couldn't ever

11

imagine myself in her place. I read Walker and Hurston and Hughes, but I also found Toni Cade Bambara and Marita Bonner and Jessie Redmon Fauset and Ernest Gaines.

Maybe I am crazy, but I didn't start out that way. Miss Ora brought out some picture albums last night, and there we were, smilin' and laughin' like nothing happened at all. We all lined up on the couch with Mama in the middle. Miss Ora called it a family portrait. Last one we ever had where we was all together – Marcus, too. It was that first Thanksgiving when we ate right here, when Marcus came home from boot camp, and Mr. Pecan was here, and I was so happy I could almost forget about that white-haired boy. And Christmas, when we made dark-skinned Santa cookies by adding cocoa to the butter cookie dough. That was the year we found bicycles under the tree. I thought the only reason we got so many presents that year was 'cause the white Santa came to Miss Ora's house, so I begged for Christmas at her house every year after that. Mama got pretty tired of it, and I think Miss Ora did, too.

Of course, none of that happiness lasted. Not even last night, with all my sisters there. Hard seeing my brother's smiling face in that first set of photos and a big empty spot where he should have been in every one afterwards. I remember him, though. His was the face I went to in my mind when I needed to know there were good men in this world. I've known precious few, and that's a sad, sorry fact.

Mind you, I've *read* about some good men, but I haven't met many. Mr. Pecan was good. And that ol' judge – even though I was scared to death of him – he was good. He helped me out some over the years, even put me in rehab a couple of times, but I didn't stay. I never stayed.

I feel like I need to go back through my whole life now. It's like I took off one pair of glasses, the ones that filtered the lie, and put on another pair that makes everything look like carnival mirrors. Hard to even get my bearings. Maybe that's why my stomach's so twisted this morning. I need to empty everything and start over.

I'll give you one good example – Miss Ora. All these years – *all* these years – I thought she was different. I know it's crazy, but I kind of looked at her like family. I thought she was the *one* white lady in this world I could trust no matter what.

Patrice and I talked about this last night. I was so mad, I could barely speak. I thought everyone knew but me and kept it from me all these years. Patrice swears she didn't, though. I asked a lot of questions. We ate here after the funeral, though there sure as hell weren't any church ladies bringin' food to a convicted murderer's family. Miss Ora got sandwich trays from Publix and Mrs. Smallwood brought a casserole. Thank God for my sisters, is all I can say. Danita cooks just like Mama did, and Re'Netta's pretty close. I didn't eat much, but I was hungrier than I expected. Miss Ora went to bed early and left us to clean up, which I guess is okay, but something about seeing Patrice standing at her sink, washing up afterwards, just went all over me.

"You ain't her maid." I set my empty glass on the counter so hard I thought I might have cracked it.

Patrice stopped, her hands covered in soap suds and dripping into the sink. She turned just her head and looked at me for a minute. She's like that. She studies things a lot. Thinks about what she's gonna say before she says it. Not me. I blurt out whatever's on my mind. Always have.

"I know I'm not, Gracie."

"And you ain't Mama, neither."

"Okay," Patrice nodded like she was thinking it over more than actually agreeing. "But these dishes aren't going to wash themselves and we ate off of them. Miss Ora's had a rough day. It won't kill us to help."

I don't know what came over me, but I started crying then. First time I've cried in I can't remember when. It don't do a thing but tear up your gut and make you look weak.

"Ain't I had a rough day, too?" I blubbered like a fool. "She don't know what rough even is, here in this lily-white house where everybody waits on her hand and foot –"

"Hush that." Danita appeared out of nowhere and wrapped her arms around me tight. She hugged me to her chest and whispered "Shhhh...shhhh...shhhh" while I cried all over her gray silk blouse.

They managed to get me to the living room and all three of my sisters sat with me until I stopped crying enough to say, "I need a drink. She got any liquor in this house?"

I don't remember when I last saw that much eye-rolling. Makes me want to roll my own eyes thinking about it.

"What?" I asked.

13

"Miss Ora doesn't keep alcohol here," Patrice said. "She used to, but she doesn't anymore, and you don't need it anyway."

"I see how this is gonna go," I said, shaking my head.

"How long you been clean this time?" Re'Netta finally spoke up. She's always the one to get things out in the open. She's like me that way.

"Most of three months now," I said, defensive as usual.

"Most of?" Patrice's head snapped up like I'd slapped her.

"It ain't easy, Sister." She's the only one I call Sister. The twins I call by their names. "Most of...meaning *most* of. At least I'm not lying about it, like everyone's been doing to me *most* of my life."

"We didn't know, Gracie," Patrice said in a way that made me believe her. "None of us knew. If I had known, I would have done things a whole lot differently."

"*She* knew," I jerked my head sideways and up, toward the stairs in the hall.

Patrice nodded again, just as Aunt Tressa came in from the front porch. I'd forgotten she was still there.

"Sorry about that," she said and held up her cell phone. "I had to check on some things back home."

"Did you know?" I asked.

"Know what?" Her eyes narrowed at me like she wasn't all that happy I was asking.

"About us. About my mama. About me."

"It's a long story, and not one to be covered in one night." She sat down ramrod straight in the recliner and leaned forward. I took that as a beginning.

4 – Patrice

I dropped the kids off at school and stopped by my office to pick up some documents I'd need to take with me to court this afternoon. I was meeting Aunt Tressa at Miss Ora's house at 10:00 a.m. and I still had a good hour to kill, so I drove aimlessly for a bit and found myself out by the prison. I pulled off the road and sat for a minute, just staring at the white concrete walls surrounded by a good mile of fences and razor wire. How did our family become so tangled in events that made *this* place part of our lives?

Last night, Aunt Tressa sat stiff and uncomfortable on an old wing chair in Ora Beckworth's living room as we waited for her to speak. She had no obligation to tell us her story, but it is one we didn't even know existed before yesterday. As it turns out, it's our story, too. Tressa Mims Hightower, daughter of Eldred and Eileen Mims, is my mother's half-sister, though as far as I can tell, Mama never knew about Tressa. Tressa, however, knew about Mama. This is what she told us last night. After Eddie's funeral. After Miss Ora dropped a few bombs on us all.

"I first learned about your mother when Eddie showed up at my house in early December of 1976. My children were just toddlers. Those would be your cousins. Trevor's 28 now and John Jackson – we've always called him JJ – is 26. They were asleep upstairs when Eddie – my father – banged on my front door begging to come in. I knew he'd been in Mayville for a good while. He said it used to be his hometown."

"Where'd you say you were from?" Grace interrupted. She never could sit still and just listen.

"We live in Auburn now. My husband teaches computer science at the university. That's not too far from Tuskegee, which is where my father was in the military and where he met my mother, and where we lived when the boys were still young."

"Mr. Pecan was in the Army?" Grace used the name she had called Eddie since the first time she met him.

"Mr. who?" Aunt Tressa asked.

"Sorry. I don't know what to call him now. He was my grandfather, right?" Grace is having the most trouble absorbing the information we just learned. I feel for her, really, I do, but sometimes it's hard to be patient with her.

"You can call him anything you like," she said. "I call him Eddie because Dad just doesn't sound right."

Grace shrugged. "I like Mr. Pecan fine. So was he, then? In the Army?"

Aunt Tressa spoke to Grace like a child, which isn't surprising. Gracie is quite childlike despite her age. "No, honey, he was a mechanic with the Tuskegee Airmen. You ever heard of them?"

Her eyes grew even larger. "Those the ones they did those tests on?"

"The very ones. I don't think Eddie had any medical issues with them. He never talked about it anyway. But that's where he got started drinking and as long as I knew him, he was a drinker. And a fighter. Hard to imagine the sweet, soft-spoken man he *was,* morphing into this loud, obnoxious character. Funny thing was, I had sent him a bus ticket to come home for the holidays, so I knew he was in town. The day he arrived, we had dinner at my house, and he sat on the floor with the boys for two hours building a train track. It was lovely, and I remember wishing it had always been that way. And then he shows up three nights later, drunk as I've ever seen him and hell-bent on telling me *something important,* he said."

Grace had this completely skeptical look going on. She doesn't have to say a word. She just wears what she's thinking on her face.

"You don't believe me?" Aunt Tressa asked Grace.

"I just don't remember ever seeing him drunk," Grace said.

"Maybe not." Tressa adjusted her skirt and sat back a bit in the chair. "But I do. Vernon – that's my husband – brought him inside and made a pot of coffee. We made him stay quiet until he drank a cup and calmed down. Then he told me about y'all. It was hard to understand at first. I was trying to calculate dates more than I was listening to what he had to say. Finally, when I realized Blanche was born before he came to Alabama, I could breathe again."

"Where was your mama all this time?" This question was from Danita. She's the compassionate one of my twin sisters. It didn't surprise me that she wanted to know about the rest of the family, too.

"She was around some, but she didn't have much interest in seeing him once they split up. She was the assistant to the president at Tuskegee. The institute became a university in the mid-eighties, which was a big deal to her, and she worked right up until the day she died.

16

She was at her office, stood up to greet a faculty member and dropped dead of a heart attack right there."

"So, what all did Mr. Pecan tell you that night?"

"Grace!" I admonished my sister. I shot her a look she's probably used to, then turned to my aunt. "I'm sorry for your loss, Aunt Tressa."

"It's fine, honey." She gave a little shake of her head to reassure me. "She just wants to know."

I relaxed then, but Grace still looked wounded, so my aunt went straight back to the story.

"He told me he had another family in Florida. Without even trying, he'd found the daughter he left when she was a baby. He had granddaughters, too, which really seemed to tickle him. He talked about you a lot, Grace. That day and every other time we talked. He told me what happened to you and how much it hurt to watch Blanche suffer. He felt guilty about her, I know that much. But this was just the first time he told me, and things were a bit fuzzy then."

"How'd he know we were his family?" I asked.

"He said the first thing he noticed was that we looked a lot alike."

"You do!" Grace chimed in. "You look just like her in the face, but Mama's face was rounder. Softer."

Aunt Tressa looked a little bemused at that, like she wasn't sure if it was a compliment or not, but she went on. "And if I remember correctly, he said something about knowing for sure when Mrs. Beckworth gave him a piece of Blanche's birthday cake one day, which makes sense. I imagine he'd remember his firstborn child's birthday. Of course, all of this happened before that boy was killed..." She stopped abruptly. I think she realized this was shaky ground for us.

I nodded. "This was before Thanksgiving then. Eddie had Thanksgiving with us."

"It was. I had planned on him staying through the holiday, but I had left his return ticket open just in case. After that night, I was ready to send him packing and I did. That kind of haunts me now. What if I had just kept him with us?" Her voice was full of emotion, and she got quiet for a moment, but I did not see tears.

I reached out to her then and placed my hand on her arm. "Let's don't do that to ourselves, okay? We all have regrets. We did what we did. Let's just let it be."

Aunt Tressa nodded and gave her body a brief shake that went all the way to her fingertips, but she got quiet then, and I got up to make a pot of coffee. It was obvious we would be talking long into the night. When I returned with five cups on a tray, I realized Grace was still grilling Aunt Tressa about Eddie.

"Did my mama know who he was?" she asked.

"I have no idea." She took the cup I offered with a grateful smile. Re'Netta relieved me of the tray and finished distributing the coffee as Tressa continued. "He said he asked Blanche about her family, but she answered only a few questions and then changed the subject."

"What questions did he ask?" Grace was determined, I'll give her that.

"Gosh, Gracie, it has been a long, long time since I even thought about this. Maybe if I'd known the significance of the details, I might have paid more attention. At the time, I was just trying to get this drunk man out of my house without risking someone else's life in the process. He probably wanted to tell me more, but I wasn't in the listening mood."

Something clicked in my brain and I blurted out. "I wondered why you didn't seem surprised when Miss Ora introduced you to us as our aunt."

She nodded. "I was a *little* surprised, but only that she knew. And that she announced it so casually."

"Were you going to tell us?" Grace frowned at Aunt Tressa. Her eyebrows were drawn into a tight knot between her enormous eyes.

"I was not," she said.

"Then you're a liar, too." Grace pronounced this as if it were a simple fact.

"I'm damned if I do and damned if I don't," she said without a trace of rancor. "Or maybe damned if I will and damned if I won't. I hadn't planned on it, Grace, but I might have once I knew you."

"But you've known *about* us all this time," Gracie said. "Why didn't you come find us?"

Tressa threw up her hands in defeat. "I can't answer that one, other than to say that it never occurred to me. It's true, I knew my father had another family in Mayville. But I had no idea they did not know him as their own. Hell, I knew nothing of his arrest, nor his arraignment, nor his guilty plea. I only found out he was in prison when he wrote me from his cell. That's how little communication I had with the man for most of my life. I rarely worried about him and never reported him missing because he always – eventually – showed up. Or at least one of

18

the money orders he sent on a fairly regular basis would arrive and I'd know he was still around. When I was in college, I cashed them right away and took them as my due. As I grew older, I saw the sacrifice for what it was. He had no court-ordered child support; my mother never divorced him. He gave what he could, and I was glad to get it. I'm not sure that I ever thought much about my father's life beyond that. God, that sounds awful..."

"Hmmph," was all Grace allowed.

Tressa sighed and leaned forward. She dropped her forehead a bit and peered intently at Grace from beneath her eyebrows. "I will tell you truthfully...right this minute I am *very* grateful Mrs. Beckworth took the decision out of my hands. I mean that."

I hadn't seen my aunt cry once since I'd met her, not even at the funeral of her father, but she got teary in that moment, which seemed to fluster her. She looked around for a tissue, I assume, and finding none, pressed at both eyes with the sides of her index fingers.

"Don't cry, Aunt Tressa." Danita was immediately off the couch and kneeling at her feet. She took both of Tressa's hands in hers and tried to console her. "We're glad, too. It's kind of like getting a piece of Mama back. We've never had an auntie before. Please don't cry."

Danita's sweetness made her cry in earnest, and she reached for her pocketbook and dug through it. That's where she found the packet of photos and letters Mrs. Beckworth had given her before the funeral. The photos were wrapped in a photocopy of some sort. I could tell by the stark white paper and the slightly rounded folds. She opened them instinctively and caught her breath.

"What is it?" I asked.

"A letter from Eddie, I guess. This is his handwriting," she pulled the pages apart and scanned them quickly.

Grace leapt from her chair and snatched the paper from Tressa's hands.

"Gracie!" I was horrified, but she was already reading the letter out loud.

19

5 ~ Eldred Mims

October 14, 1999

Dear Miss Ora,

If you're reading this, I must be gone. I'm feeling my age now, and I'm weary. I'm looking forward to going home. There was some talk of a new parole hearing, but I know they won't release me. I'm talking about going home to the Lord. I know he has prepared a table for me there, and isn't that a comforting thought? I pray for you and the girls a lot. It just about killed me not to go to Blanche's funeral. Patrice still comes by to see me now and then, and that's a blessing. I guess you're wondering why I'm writing this letter. I got to thinking about what they would do with me when I die, and where they'd put my stuff, what little they is of it. So I told Mr. Chip to please pack everything up and take it to your house. Including my ashes if that's what they inclined to do. Maybe they'll bury me, and that's fine, too. I just don't want nobody bearing the cost of it, you neither. I read my Bible a lot in here. It's the one you give me right after I came out to the prison. I don't take to the trash they pass off as books in this place. Bible got all the stories I need now. But it got me to thinking about things I done over the years. Remember I told you this one time before, sometimes the debt you pay ain't exactly the one you owe, but it works out just the same. I done a lot wrong, and I know God forgive me. I know He do, sure as I know the sun rise every day.

They's something I need to get off my chest, though, and I'm disinclined to talk about it before I die. But I don't want it dying with me if it brings the truth to light. People gots a right to know from whence they came, even if they already know who they are down inside.

Miss Ora, I done bad things in my life. Real bad things. I run away from not one daughter, but two, and only one of them even knew I was they daddy. I left my family for the bottle too many times to count. I left two women who was good women. Way too good to take up with the likes of me, and yet both of them was faithful and true and loved me more than I deserved. And I repaid them by leaving them to raise babies

20

by theyself. What kind of man is this? A broken man, that's what. And yet God's gonna make me whole again soon. And it's that kind of grace and mercy makes me want to do better. I don't know if this is right, but I know it's true. I'm leaving this confession in your lap, and I hope you'll forgive me, too, but I'm leaving it on your heart to do what you will with it. Blanche Lowery my daughter. I'm them girls' granddaddy. That's why I done what I done. If I was the man I should have been, ain't none of this would've happened. May God have mercy on my soul.

October 20, 1999

I had to stop writing for a while, but I come back to it now. That took it all out of me. I was shaking too hard to even hold my pen. I left Blanche's mama when she was just a few days old. I was young and stupid and mostly scared half to death, but I was also mean-hearted. We wasn't married and not even living together, 'cause she didn't care to live in sin. How was I to know who that baby father was? But I did know. I just gave myself a pass to leave it all behind. I heard about the Tuskegee airmen over in Alabama, and I hopped a train first chance I got.

They 'bout didn't take me, but I knew engines and motors and fixing broke things from working on farms and in the orange groves most of my life. I drawed a diagram of an idea I had to convert an old steam tractor to gas and they finally agreed to test me for service. I wanted so bad to fly, but my eyes failed me there. I was happy to be around those airplanes, though, and it didn't take long to just plain forget about that baby and her mama. You want to know the sad truth about that? I never even knowed her name until I met her that day on your porch. I didn't know she was my daughter then. I just knew she looked mighty familiar.

Anyway, I had me a new life out in Alabama and it was mostly good. I was feeling pretty good about myself working on them planes. Kind of a hotshot I reckon. I met Tressa's mama and she wouldn't give me the time of day 'til she had a ring on her finger. We was married 'fore I knew it, and Tressa borned a year later. I was good for a while, but there was a lotta drinking on that base. Lotta drinking. I ain't going into all them details. Tressa knows that story and she can tell you what she likes. I helped her when I could. I didn't half the time have a roof over my head when the war was over, but I sent her what I could manage.

21

She was set on going to college and I was gonna help her get there. I would have gone myself if I could have, but we was still under Jim Crow down here and the G.I. bill didn't do me no good when they wasn't a college would take me. But I was proud of Tressa, just like I'm proud of Patrice, and I want her to know that.

I reckon I gone on long enough, Miss Ora. I don't want you feeling guilty about nothing, you hear me? What's done is done. Blanche is gone and I'll be gone soon, too. If you gone before me, Mr. Chip knows to give this to Patrice in your stead. They's one more thing I'm gonna ask you, though. I done worried myself sick about little Gracie. That child got thrown asunder in all this. I ain't faulting you or Blanche for it, but it ain't that child's fault neither. And it ain't her fault she all wrapped up in them drugs. She needs help, Miss Ora. She needs help like I shoulda got long ago myself, but she needs it worse than I ever did. I want you to tell her she a good child. She got the best heart of them all, and she ought to know she mean everything to her ol' granddaddy, for whatever that's worth. Please tell her I love her. Please tell her I'm sorry for it all.

Eddie

6 – Patrice

I took one last look at the prison where Eldred Mims died, and felt an overwhelming mix of sadness and anger. So many things make sense now. I rested my forehead against the steering wheel and wept for the third time in a week. I don't usually give in to emotions; they don't work in my favor in a courtroom. But, damn it all, I could have fixed this. Maybe not in the beginning, but certainly before it went this far.

I found a clean napkin in my center console and blew my nose. I'm not one to complain. What good does it do, anyway? My life, despite a few hardships, has been blessed. I had the love of a good, strong mother, a brother I adored, and three younger sisters to laugh with over the years, and cry with when we suffered those terrible losses. I had a benefactor who made sure I got through college – Miss Ora hounded the hell out of me if she thought I was making bad choices. I did make a few of those over the years, and still made it out virtually unscathed.

I put my car in drive and pulled away from the chain link fence I'd been staring through. I had twenty minutes to get back to Miss Ora's house and that's about what it would take. I got the fleeting thought that I would see Mama when I got there. I haven't gotten used to those little blips in the brain, and the muscle memories, that make you think and rethink in an instant. Before you can even smile you remember that she isn't there anymore. And then your brain fully engages and you remember everything.

I have watched my sister, for years now, make one bad decision after the other. My mother rationalized every single one. While I was buying Mama a new washer and dryer, or clothes for Shawn and Rochelle, she was sending Grace money for drugs. In her mind she was helping her daughter pay bills, or go to the doctor, or put food on the table; she was doing for her child what Miss Ora did for me. Except, she was not. It was *not* the same, and I couldn't convince her of this. She quoted the Bible at me when the truth hit too close to home to argue.

"All y'all spend too much time judgin' the other," she said. "So busy pointing out the speck in your brother's eye, you can't see the log in your own."

"What log, Ma?" I screamed at her one time. "Show me the log!"

23

I hated arguing with my mother, and now that she is gone, I regret it even more. I've forgiven her, of course, but it's not that simple with my sister. Knowing what she went through makes it more complicated, for sure, but it doesn't take away the anger. She caused turmoil in my family, and she is not blameless. At some point, you have to recognize that none of the pain inflicted on you gives you the right to hurt others. At some point, you have to step up and take care of yourself, instead of abdicating all responsibility for your actions and their consequences.

I am *so* sad knowing what Gracie went through. I can't even imagine what it has been like for her. And yet, I *can* imagine, because I know firsthand what it's been like for us. And it has been hell. Pure hell.

So, despite my anger at her, last night, when Gracie broke down over Eddie's letter, I totally got it. She was distraught. So was I, and so were my sisters – knowing what Eddie did for us. His sacrifice was astounding. It comes with a weight that is almost too much to bear.

And Gracie's wailing was proof of the unbearable. It woke Miss Ora and she rushed into the room still trying to tie her robe around her waist.

We had swaddled Gracie in one of Miss Ora's blankets and she lay curled in an almost fetal position between the twins on the couch. Her eyes were closed, but tears poured sideways down her face and her wail had reduced to a soft moan. I was kneeling in front of her trying to make her sip some water; Tressa was sitting in the recliner not saying much at all.

"Gracie, listen to me," I kept saying. "You have to snap out of this. Drink this water. Drink it, Gracie. Drink the water."

Danita was stroking her head and whispering something I couldn't hear. Re'Netta had her hand on Grace's leg and was pushing her back and forth…almost like rocking a cradle.

"What is it?" Miss Ora asked by way of announcing her presence. "What in the world happened?"

Tressa stood then. "I found Eddie's letter and she read it. I think it was just more than she could take."

I was getting more frustrated, which only made Gracie moan louder.

Miss Ora tried to diffuse the situation. "Patrice, honey, why don't you go make some coffee and just let her be for a minute?"

Something in me snapped. I spun my head sideways and looked up at her over my shoulder.

"Are you kidding me?" I asked.

24

"I'm sorry," she stammered. "I just thought... She needs to rest a minute, Patrice. Maybe if you just let her alone –"

"*Please* don't tell me how to handle my sister, Miss Ora. Please don't. I've been handling her *all* my *life* without your input. I think I know what I'm doing." I stood then and faced her with my fists balled up tight and resting on my hips.

"It isn't working, though." She trailed off and pulled at her belt again.

"You don't have to tell me it's not working, Miss Ora." I flung one hand behind me and pointed at my sister, still huddled on the couch. "It hasn't been working for years now, because *she* makes *everything* about herself."

"Patrice, don't," Danita said, covering Grace's exposed ear with one hand.

I wheeled to face my sister. "That's what Mama always said. *Patrice, don't.* Ain't nobody saying 'Grace, don't,' though. *Nobody* is saying 'Grace, don't expect everybody to take care of you and your children. Grace, don't kill yourself with those drugs.' They say, 'Patrice, don't make a fuss. Shawn and Rochelle need you.' Well, I know they need me. But they need me because their own mother won't take care of *herself*, much less *them*."

I started to feel weak then, and my heart was pounding in my chest.

Tressa spoke up then and, for a second, I wondered if she was just confused and calling me by the wrong name. "Mrs. Beckworth, are you okay?"

"I don't feel well," Miss Ora said.

I squinted my eyes and examined her face.

"Miss Ora, you're white as a sheet," I came to my senses and took her by the arm.

"Take her upstairs," Aunt Tressa ordered, as if she'd been doing it all of our lives. "I'll be up in a minute."

I did as I was told, and carefully guided her up the stairs to her bed. I got her a glass of water and sat with her until she said she felt better.

"I'm sorry I yelled at you," I said after a while.

She shook her head. "You didn't yell."

"I know, but I wasn't very nice, and I really am sorry."

She reached up and laid her hand on my arm. It was cold and so pale, I could see right through her skin. Her veins were purple and one of them bulged up near her wrist and split into a Y at her ring finger. It was such a contrast against my dark skin, that I couldn't help taking notice of it. I covered her hand with my own and tried to warm it.

She squeezed my hand in response. "Patrice, you have nothing to apologize to me for. Nothing at all."

"I've been doing this a long time, Miss Ora. I've been the fix-it person for so long, and I don't know how to fix this."

"Let it mend itself, honey. You didn't break it," she said.

I nodded and fell silent. We sat like that for a long time more, until Tressa came up to tell us she had given Gracie something to make her sleep and tucked her into bed.

7 – Grace

I wasn't sure exactly when Patrice and Aunt Tressa would arrive the next morning, but I dared not make myself too comfortable. I'd never hear the end of it from Sister if I was in bed when she got here. She wouldn't believe I'd already been up. She don't believe anything I say anymore.

I took a quick shower and put on the same clothes I wore to the funeral yesterday. They clean enough, I guess, but I'll be glad to get a few things from Mama's house when I can. Aunt Tressa brought me a pair of pajamas with the sleeping pill she gave me last night. Must be Miss Ora's 'cause they fit just fine. Tressa's way taller'n me, so they couldn't be hers.

When I went back to the kitchen, the backyard caught my eye and I stepped outside to breathe. I hated seeing that yard in such a state. Everything was overgrown. I went to the garage and found a pair of pruning shears that still had sharp edges. Then I got busy. The camellias were long past just dead-heading. I cut them all the way back. The azaleas around her oak tree were halfway up the trunk, though, so I thought I'd better go find a pair of loppers before digging into that mess. That's when I saw Eddie's chair pushed over in the corner of the garage and half-covered by a blue tarp. I made a lot of noise walkin' up to it, just in case some little mousies were keepin' house under there. I pulled back the tarp and dust rolled in waves through the light streaming in the side window. It's still a beautiful thing, that old barber's chair, even though it's covered in a half inch of dust and the base has gone all rusty. I remember helpin' Mr. Pecan polish this thing. He woulda never let it get this bad.

I thought about that letter I read last night. I never cried so hard in my life. Not even when Mama died, which I still ain't over. I never knew Marcus killed that white boy until Miss Ora told us yesterday. I always thought Mr. Pecan did it 'cause why else would he confess? So now, on top of all this mess of lies and plain trippin' in my head over what's dream and what's real, I gotta wrestle with knowing that old man went to jail for something he ain't even done. I never knew love that big.

27

I loved Mr. Pecan. I remember following him around like a little puppy. Wherever he went, I was right behind him. He taught me how to prune roses and how to fix the chain on my bike. He taught me how to play marbles and mumbly peg, which my mama wasn't none too happy about. She didn't want me playin' with knifes, no matter how small. I don't know why I didn't go see him when he was out at that prison. Well, I guess I do know why. I was kind of afraid if I went I'd never come back.

I don't think I'll ever sort this out. Mr. Pecan knew, too, and he didn't tell me. All he had to do is just whisper to me one time – *it ain't a dream, child. It happened to you.* That's all he had to do and he didn't do it, neither.

But I can't think about all that right now. I gotta figure out a way to keep going. I been clean longer than I usually make it, and I'm stayin' with Miss Ora. I got Patrice and my sisters and my kids to live for and didn't none of *them* know what happened to me. I just gotta have an *attitude* of *gratitude.* That's what they used to say in one of the rehabs. I remember thinking…huh, yeah…I'll be grateful when I get outta this place, dude. That's when I'll be grateful. Still, sometimes it works.

8 – Patrice

Aunt Tressa and I arrived at Mrs. Beckworth's house at 10:00 a.m. on the dot. Grace was out in the backyard tending the garden. I stood at the kitchen window and watched my sister bent over a copse of tea roses with a pair of pruning scissors in her hand. She held each stem she cut by the outermost leaves, then dropped the pruned section into a five-gallon bucket at her feet. The morning sun illuminated her face and, for the first time in years, I saw my sister as I remember her from childhood. She looked up then, and I moved away from the window and stepped onto the porch to wave her in. Aunt Tressa followed.

"Hey!" Grace met us with childlike exuberance, as if nothing had happened the night before. She hugged me tight, holding her body against mine a few moments longer than a casual greeting.

"I love you so much," she said just before letting go.

I felt myself relax then, like yielding in a way, not bracing like I'd done for months – no – years now.

She gave Aunt Tressa a quick hug and laughed when she realized she still held the pruning shears.

"You look right at home in that backyard," Aunt Tressa said.

Grace smiled and nodded. "I kinda grew up here. Mr. Pecan taught me how to tend flowers and I took over for him when he went away. The camellias are overgrown and the roses are a little rangy, but not as bad as I thought they'd be. Last time I was here was two years ago. They don't get the attention they used to, but I'll get 'em back into shape."

Aunt Tressa squinted at her. "In one day?"

Grace laughed. "No, Miss Ora wants me to stay here a while." She shrugged like it was out of her hands, and we entered the kitchen together. Miss Ora was still at the kitchen table, reading her morning paper.

"For how long?" I asked Grace.

"I don't know. Ask her yourself," Grace said.

Miss Ora looked up at me. "I hope it's okay, Patrice. I should have spoken to you first."

"It certainly isn't up to me," I said, more sharply than I intended. "She has options."

"Speaking of options..." Miss Ora has an odd way about her, ignoring tension like it isn't there. My mama, on the other hand, might not have called me out on my tone, but I'd have known real quick that she noticed and disapproved. Miss Ora just glossed right over my sarcasm like it was sincerity. "Why don't we move to the dining room for a minute. I have a few things I'd like to discuss with all of you. Legal things, so I think it's best to get this out of the way while Tressa is still here."

We migrated to Miss Ora's long mahogany table which had obviously been prepared in advance. There were four places set with delicate teacups and saucers, and a plate of butter cookies beside an ornate silver tea service in the center of the table. My sisters used to love helping Miss Ora polish that set. Despite the nostalgia, I couldn't help feeling a little ambushed.

Miss Ora took her place at the head of the table. She looked frail and shaky, despite being dressed in a suit I hadn't seen her wear in years.

"As you just heard," she began, "I've asked Gracie to stay with me for a while. I feel like it will be mutually beneficial in the long run. I haven't been feeling myself lately, and I could use some company at the very least, and possibly a little assistance, though she is certainly under no obligation to me whatsoever. I have no idea how long it will be, of course..."

Her voice seemed to catch and she cleared her throat and reached for the teapot. Her hands shook so badly she spilled water onto the table before she even reached her cup. She set the pot back onto the tray and sat down looking a little bewildered. Aunt Tressa, sitting immediately to Miss Ora's right, slid the linen napkin from beneath the silverware at her place setting and mopped up the spill before it did any damage.

"Here, let me," she said, and filled all of our cups with steaming water.

"I don't know when I started getting so clumsy," Miss Ora said.

I busied myself with the teabag. Grace ignored the water in her cup and plunged onward. "How long it will be until what?"

"Well, until I'm gone, I suppose."

"Are you dyin' or something?" Grace asked.

Miss Ora gave a little laugh. "Well, eventually, I suppose, but that's not exactly what I meant. Clara Jean took my formal confession. I'm

30

planning on taking it to the state attorney's office," she began. "I have no idea what will happen with that. I'm waiting to hear from Clara Jean that it's been transcribed."

"Why are you calling it a confession, Miss Ora?" Grace sat forward in her chair and braced both hands against the table. "You didn't do nothin' wrong."

"Oh, but I did," Ora looked at me for confirmation, I thought, and I gave a non-committal shrug in response. It's not for me to decide. "I destroyed evidence in a criminal case at the very least."

"What evidence?" Grace demanded.

"Calm down, Grace." I shoved the cookies toward my sister. "Eat some cookies and just listen."

"I'm not a child." Grace reached for the cookies anyway.

"I'm not saying what I did was wrong – God can judge that – but it was certainly against the law. If I had it to do over again, I doubt I would have done differently. I've made peace with my choices. We all did what we did and we have to live with the consequences. Mine may well be that I go to prison, and I'm prepared to do that." Grace stiffened and shook her head, but Miss Ora held up both hands to silence her and went on. "Yours, Gracie, have been far more devastating. We did *not* handle your situation well." She lifted a note pad from the sideboard behind her and set it down beside her place setting. "That's why I have a proposal that I feel suits everyone's needs at this time."

I think Aunt Tressa was the most surprised when Miss Ora revealed what she and I had discussed months before. She was leaving her house to my sisters and me. I was a little confused, though. From the sounds of it, she was not planning on waiting until she was gone.

"Are you sure that's a good idea?" Aunt Tressa asked.

I didn't take her question personally. I was still considering the implications of her news. But Grace frowned at her for a brief second. I don't think Aunt Tressa noticed. She was looking intently at Miss Ora.

"I've discussed it with my personal attorney. It will be in a trust at first, with Patrice and I as co-trustees. We have a contingency plan in place if that becomes necessary," Miss Ora said, "but I don't think it will. I just need to get my ducks in a row while I still can."

"Where will you go?" Aunt Tressa asked.

"She's not going anywhere right now," I interrupted. "She's staying right here."

31

Aunt Tressa looked back and forth between Miss Ora and me several times, as if she were weighing what she was about to say and to whom she would say it. She finally settled on Miss Ora. "Didn't I just understand you to say that the transfer of the deed is imminent, Mrs. Beckworth?"

"Oh, please, can we just dispense with the formalities?" Miss Ora slid the linen napkin out from under her teaspoon and dabbed at the corners of her mouth. "Call me Ora. I still think of my mother-in-law when I hear 'Mrs. Beckworth,' and that is not altogether a positive association, God rest her soul."

Aunt Tressa laughed. "Fair enough. Ora it is."

"So wait," I said, "you're transferring ownership – like – now?"

"We already talked about this," Ora said. "We're transferring it to the family trust."

I probably could have handled this better, but I was not in the mood to be patronized, to be honest. "I know that," I snapped, "but I didn't know it would happen this soon. I don't want to be rude, but I have a lot on my plate right now."

The silence in the room was palpable. Miss Ora's mouth hung open for a brief moment before her manners kicked in and she closed it with a click of her teeth. Aunt Tressa broke the tension by placing her hand gently over mine.

"Is there anything I can do to help?" she asked.

"I'm sorry," I was immediately contrite. "I'm just overwhelmed."

"I think we all are," she agreed, then added without considering her words, "This whole thing has been a case of information overload."

A wave of realization washed over Miss Ora's face, staining her face and neck a bright pink.

"Oh, Lord...what was I thinking?" She clasped both hands to her cheeks and sank into her chair. "It just never occurred to me that I might be telling too much too soon."

Grace piped up then. "May be a fine line between too much, too soon, and too little, too late. I'm guessing it depends on where you're standin'."

I glared at her and shook my head. Really, she can be so thoughtless sometimes. Grace shrugged and picked at her fingernails. "I'm just sayin'..."

Miss Ora seemed to shrink in her chair. I thought she was going to speak, but she didn't. She just stared at Grace, who did not look up from her hands.

"So where do we go from here?" Aunt Tressa asked after another moment of awkward silence.

I looked over at Grace and saw her freeze. It was like she knew I was watching her and refused to breathe until I looked away. I wondered for a moment what it must have felt like for Grace to have been cast aside like she was. She was betrayed, but it wasn't by me. And still – there she sits, waiting for the next rebuke, the next reason to feel like nobody cares. She looked up then and caught my eye. She sat up straight and fixed me with a gaze I could not read. I turned to Aunt Tressa, but still said nothing.

She tried again. "I told my husband I wasn't coming home right away. I feel like I might be needed here, but I don't want to intrude."

"I would appreciate your help." I said, and felt my shoulders drop with relief.

"I would, too," Miss Ora said. "Lord knows I've made a mess of things as it is."

Grace was non-committal. "Whatever works for y'all."

Aunt Tressa took the reins then, and we made a list of questions going forward. We had legal concerns and logistical ones. We had no idea what the state's attorney would do with Ora's confession, and that caused a stir in itself. It was the only time Grace didn't sit there looking bored.

"When will you know what the prosecutor will do with the case?" Aunt Tressa directed this question at me, apparently assuming I had been involved in the confession.

"I have no idea," I responded. "Clara handled all that."

"Remind me who Clara is?" Aunt Tressa said. "I remember hearing the name yesterday."

"Clara Jean Smallwood," Ora replied. "She used to work for Judge Odell, who was a personal friend of mine. She transcribed my confession."

Grace flung her hands into her lap as if they were gloves she'd just peeled off and not cuticles. "I wish you would stop calling it a confession, Miss Ora. You didn't kill nobody."

"No, but I covered up a crime – though I'm still not sure I consider what Marcus did a crime at all. In my mind, it was self-defense. He didn't start that fight. He just finished it."

I had questions about my brother's involvement with Skipper's death, but I wasn't ready to ask them just yet. Marcus wasn't just my brother, he was my best friend, and not a day goes by that I don't mourn his absence.

Aunt Tressa had no way of knowing how raw it still was for me and asked a perfectly reasonable question. "What exactly happened? I never heard the whole story."

"This may not be the time to go into all that," Ora said. "Suffice it to say that Skipper Kornegay's body had over twenty wounds, all inflicted by his own knife, but wielded by Marcus Lowery."

I immediately felt nauseous and slumped in my seat. Grace leaned forward in her chair, all ears. Miss Ora paused and seemed to be considering what to say next. She drew her lips into a thin line, closed her eyes and breathed in through her nose. I thought she held her breath for an extraordinary amount of time, and when she finally exhaled, she gave this account:

"When Marcus showed up at my house covered in blood, he told me what happened and I believed him. I believe him to this day. He ran into Skipper by accident and they had words. Marcus confronted him and Skipper not only admitted what he'd done, he *taunted* Marcus – mocked him – then chased him into the woods. He would have killed him, I'm certain of that. Skipper pulled a knife and attacked your brother." She looked directly at me when she said this. "Which, of course, was foolish. Marcus was always a strong, athletic boy, but he was near the end of basic training. He'd never been more prepared for a fight than at that moment. He fought back and won. I want you to know something though. Your brother was...he was one of the most honorable young men I've ever known. He was distraught. He had taken another boy's life. And whether or not it was self-defense, Marcus knew he'd been motivated by an anger and hatred he didn't know he was capable of bearing. This boy, who mocked him and called him a horrible name. This boy, who raped his baby sister –"

Grace made a choking sound and covered her face with both hands. Ora's voice shook with emotion as she continued.

"I'm sorry, Gracie. Marcus loved you so much." She picked up a napkin and clenched it in one hand. "I knew I had to get him out of town. I needed to at least buy some time. I meant to spare Blanche more trauma, but if I'm honest with myself, I know I would have done anything – anything – to keep Marcus out of prison." Ora could not go on. She covered her mouth with the napkin, coughed a couple of times and then dabbed at her eyes.

"And his name was never brought up with regard to the Kornegay case?" Tressa asked.

"Not to my knowledge," Ora answered. "The Kornegay boy was missing for a couple of days, which nearly killed me. I was about to blow the whole thing when they found his body. It had rained hard the night before, so there was very little evidence at the scene."

"What about the knife?"

"I don't know. I never thought to ask about that."

It was too much. Too much. I stood abruptly and excused myself.

"Sister," Grace reached out as I passed, but I sidestepped and avoided her grasp.

"Let her go," I heard Ora say as I stepped into the kitchen. "She just needs a minute."

I could hear them discussing the details of the case, with Grace asking question after question, but I didn't want to be in the room. When it seemed they were winding down, I poured myself a glass of water and rejoined them at the dining room table.

Aunt Tressa waited for me to sit down and then changed the subject. "I've been thinking about something, and I'm not really sure how to approach it, so I think I'll just hit it head on. This family, myself included, has suffered unthinkable trauma, both over the years and in the past few days."

Miss Ora covered her face with her hands.

"Ora, you did what you thought was right. I want you to hear me," Aunt Tressa waited for Ora to look at her.

"I'm listening," she said.

"I'm not criticizing you at all. What happened, happened. Nothing can be undone. But we all need each other right now, and we all need counseling. I've done a little work over the years trying to come to terms with my absentee father, but so much has changed, I don't even know what to think, and I'm the least affected of *all* of us.

And the thing is," she continued, "I think we need *family* counseling to get through this. I'm sitting here looking at family I'd like to know better, but I'm afraid I'll walk away from here and never see any of you

35

again. There is so much good that can come of these revelations, and yet there is so much that can destroy us all, especially Grace, and I, for one, cannot bear the thought."

"I'm already destroyed, Aunt Tressa," Grace said without looking up.

"I see that," she replied. "But I promise you, Gracie...look at me. I promise you, we'll get help for you. There must be some residential facilities close by..."

"See," Grace interrupted. "That's y'all's idea of help. Get rid of the problem by sending it away."

Miss Ora flinched like she'd been slapped. "Gracie, no, that's not what she meant. Tressa, tell her."

Aunt Tressa did not speak. I could tell she was weighing her words. I do the same thing sometimes.

"I'm not staying in another one of those places," Grace shook her head vehemently. "Last time I went, I met the guy who made me relapse when I got out."

"Made you?" I scoffed. "Like you don't have any control over your own choices?"

"Actually, Sister, I do have control," Grace snarled right back. "I'm not going."

"Okay," Aunt Tressa said. "Looks like we have a stalemate. Maybe we should consider some other options."

I looked over at Miss Ora, who was obviously deep in thought.

"Well then," she said, her face lighting up ridiculously as she spoke. "We'll just have to bring the mountain to Muhammed."

I scrunched my face into a tight grimace and tried to interpret her statement.

"Well, really," Ora said. "I've been wondering what to do with the rest of my estate. The scholarship program is funded for the next twenty years. Shawn and Rochelle have their own college accounts, which Patrice administers. We can do some kind of rehab center here. Grace can be our first resident. We'll do family counseling, too. All of us, Shawn and Rochelle, especially. I won't transfer the title immediately and that will take some pressure off Patrice. But the girls will still get the house when I'm gone."

And so a plan was hatched, an idea set into motion, without any clue if it was feasible, or if Muhammed would ever get well.

9 – Grace

I left the table while they were still making plans for my rehab center. It won't surprise me if Miss Ora names it after me and thinks she's done something good. I swear to God that woman would meddle with the devil. They all would, come to think of it, but Miss Ora takes the damn cake. It's hard for me to be mad at her, same as it's hard to be mad at my mama, but seriously, these people can just push me over the edge sometimes.

I walked outside to get some air; it was getting a little hard to breathe. I heaved open the garage door and saw the chair sitting right where I left it. Miss Ora need to get a car, I'm just sayin'. Big ol' empty space where a car ought to be, just sittin' there beggin' to be filled.

I pulled and pushed and rolled that old chair right smack dab in the middle of it. There was still a box of old rags in a bucket under the workbench, so I pulled a few out, shook them hard and wiped down the chair as best I could. Then I sat down, leaned back onto the headrest and thought about what Aunt Tressa said. She's right, I think. It's possible she could walk out of here today and never see us again. If Miss Ora goes to prison... If Patrice cuts me out of my kids' lives... If I go back to the street... Won't take much to upset the apple cart, as Mama used to say. But I think that's just dumb. This apple cart done spilt all over the   street, and I can't imagine any kind of counseling that's gonna set it right again.

But I'm go'n do the damn counseling anyway, even if it's only to shut them the hell up. I know I got a problem, but it ain't one they'll ever understand.

You know what that boy did to me? It's one of the few things I remember clear as if it happened yesterday. He had me down on the ground – this was *after* he done his business – he was holdin' me down by my arms. I was cryin' still, but not screamin', 'cause he covered my mouth and nose when I screamed and I couldn't breathe. He told me to shut the hell up and he'd let me go, so I shut up. I'm six damn years old, and I sucked up my tears, choked 'em down my throat, and stared up at him. He just looked at me then...didn't say nothin' at all for the longest time. So I said, "I'm quiet. You go'n let me up?" He didn't answer. He just spit in my face and started laughin'. That's the one thing I won't never forget. That boy spittin' in my face like I was the dirt I was layin' in. What rehab go'n do to fix that? That's what I wanna know.

10 – Patrice

After our meeting, Miss Ora went upstairs to rest. Aunt Tressa and I cleaned up and chatted over another cup of coffee. Neither of us was in a hurry to get anywhere, though I did have an appointment later in the day. Aunt Tressa asked how I was holding up and it was all I could do to keep it together just long enough to answer the question.

"Overwhelmed," I said.

"You have every reason to be," she said. "Every reason in the world."

"The thing is, whether Skipper Kornegay deserved it or not, it is a horrible thought that our sweet, kind brother, who never so much as raised his voice at us in anger, took another boy's life."

"I wish I had known him," Aunt Tressa said.

I nodded. "I wish you had, too. He was..." I couldn't go on. The lump in my throat was a boulder. I took a sip of coffee trying to wash it down. "He was amazing," I finished.

"I believe that," she said. "Makes me all the more distressed that I didn't know my sister, either."

I laughed. "Mama was something else. I think you would have liked her, but she was closed off sometimes. Hard to read. Knowing her, I think she would have been half impressed and half intimidated by you."

"Really?" Aunt Tressa stared out the kitchen window for a moment. Her eyes were half-closed and she had almost, but not quite, a smile on her face. I'd seen that same look on my mother's face more times than I could count. "I wonder why."

I laughed then. "Same reason she kept reminding me not to get too full of myself. She was proud, but I have a hunch she just felt left behind sometimes."

"What about Gracie?" she asked. "What was she like before all this?"

"Oh, gosh," I said, "she was the funniest kid. Everybody loved Gracie."

"When did it start going wrong for her, then? Was she okay after Marcus died? How'd she take his death?"

I took a deep breath and thought about that. I shook my head and frowned. "I don't actually remember a lot about that time. Not about Gracie, anyway. I was so busy at school and with my own grief. Grace stayed here with Miss Ora and Mama in the afternoons and I'd ride my bike home after cheerleading practice. I was almost done with college by the time it really started going bad."

"I'm curious to know if Grace ever talked about the rape at all. Seems odd that you never had a clue."

"Yeah, and that bothers me a lot now, knowing what Grace went through, and the awfulness of our mother's lie. I remember the nightmares because they happened all the time. She would say "that white-haired boy was after me" and I remember at one point assuming she meant Skipper. He was the only white-headed boy I knew. But that's as far as it went for me. I never connected the two of them physically because I never knew she was hurt."

"But she had nightmares a lot?" Aunt Tressa asked.

"Lord, yes," I said. "She used to wake up screaming bloody murder and Mama would rock her and tell her it was just a dream. I can hear her now. 'Just a dream, child, just a dream.' How could she do that?"

Aunt Tressa didn't respond and we sat in silence for a moment

"Know what else is crazy?" I said. "He was a year behind me at school. I'd known him since fifth grade, when our schools were first integrated. He was a bully and everyone knew it, and yet it was still a big deal when he died. We had prayer meetings for him at the flagpole, and an entire assembly was dedicated to his memory. We planted a tree outside the front gates of the school and had fundraisers to pay for the plaque we laid in the ground at its base. I personally bought ribbon to cover the tree in blue bows because someone said it was his favorite color. The crazy thing is, even kids who couldn't stand him were all a sudden acting like he was a hero, and all he did was die. And my mama knew this was going on and never stopped me from participating. Again, all I can ask is: How could she *do* that?"

"Maybe she was just doing the only thing she knew how to do," Aunt Tressa said, "which is just sad to me. I can't even imagine thinking the only option you had was to suffer in silence."

"I think that's what she expected us all to do," I said, but I think I was mostly talking about Grace.

11 – Grace

I found Aunt Tressa and Sister sitting at the kitchen table when I finally went back in. "You got time to run me home to get some clothes? I need to get out of these 'fore they walk away by themselves."

"I do," she said, "but we'll have to be quick. I have to be in court at three."

So, we made plans to meet her back here tonight for supper. Apparently Miss Ora invited them all, though I don't know who she thinks is gonna cook, 'cause I have my limits in that department.

On the ride over, Sister was pretty quiet. I'm used to gettin' the silent treatment from her. Sometimes it's 'cause she's mad. Other times it's just she don't know what to say, I guess.

"So what's your court case about?" I asked when the silence got to me.

"What?" Patrice looked sideways at me.

"This afternoon...what's the case about?"

"Oh," she said. "Just a VOP and a DUI plea. Nothing big."

"What he do to violate?" I asked.

She hesitated a second before she spoke, like she was going to say something else and changed her mind. "Failed a drug test," she said.

"You're lyin'," I said and turned away from her in my seat.

"Why would I lie about that?" she asked.

"Can you just stop? Why do you do that?" I leaned my head against the cool glass of the passenger window.

"Okay, okay," she said, "but he is on parole for drugs. He didn't show up for counseling two weeks in a row. I'm figuring Judge Milford will send him back. She's hardline on those things."

I'm so tired of this. Everything she says is aimed at fixing me, warning me, scaring me. And she wonders why I roll my eyes at her all the time. It's just stupid how she does.

"If you're trying to scare me, Sister, it isn't working. First of all, I'm not on drugs. You can go grab a drug test right now and I'll pass it. And second of all, I'm not afraid of going back to jail, so you can just stop. You think you and Miss Ora any better than prison guards? Think

41

again. It's all bars and busts and *behave yourself, Grace*. No damn difference, trust me."

Patrice pulled into the tiny dirt driveway at Mama's old house. "Need some help getting your stuff?"

"No thanks, don't put yourself out on my account," I said and got out of the car.

I was folding underwear and stacking them into a corner of Mama's old brown suitcase when Patrice appeared in my bedroom door. I almost said Mama's bedroom.

"Grace," she leaned against the door jam, "I owe you an apology."

"For what?" I asked, not contradicting her – just wondering which apology I was about to get.

"For everything," she said.

"Well, that covers a lot," I smiled, but I'm not sure I actually thought it was funny.

"Mostly for assuming the worst all the time, although I have to say, you can't always blame me. It's not like I don't have history directing my thoughts."

"That's not an apology, Sister." I grabbed several t-shirts from the shelf in the closet and threw them in beside my underwear. I had no pajamas like Aunt Tressa put me in last night. I've got sweat pants and t-shirts and usually I just sleep in the shirts. Wonder how that's gonna fly on Main Street.

"Then let me ask you this," Patrice said, straightening the shirts I just put in. "Do *you* think I owe you one?"

I looked up at her then. I'm so tired of fighting.

"I'm not asking for an apology, Sister. You offered it."

"Yeah, I did," she said, "and I meant it. I'm sorry for what you have been through. I'm sorry Mama lied to you. I'm sorry you think I'm a prison guard, because that is not what I intend."

I shook my head, "I know, I know...that was mean."

"I want to help you, Gracie. But I'm not sure how to do that."

"You are helping me," I said, and I meant it. Hell, I'd be awful not to think that. She's raising my kids.

"I'm certainly trying to. I'm doing the best I can, but..."

Here it comes. If she's waiting for me to say "but, what?" she go'n wait a good long while. "You wanna take this on out to the car?" I zipped up the suitcase and handed it to her. "I'm gonna grab my hang-up clothes and I'll be right out."

"That's okay," Patrice said, a big ol' smug-ass smile on her face, like she caught me tryin' to do something. "I'll walk out with you."

My eyes gonna roll out my head one of these days. She think she know so much.

"Suit yourself," I said.

"How long you think you'll be staying with Miss Ora?" Sister asked.

I shrugged. "Who knows? She say she just want company, but I'm not so sure. I ain't nobody's maid."

Sister frowned. "I don't think she means that, but really, it won't hurt you to help her a little."

"She go'n fall down those stairs one of these days, way she moves. She need to switch rooms with me or something. I'll help her do that, but I'm tellin' you now, I'm not there to wait on her hand and foot like Mama did."

"No one expects you to, Grace."

That's Sister for you. That is one loaded statement right there. She wrong to think I don't know what she means.

12 – Patrice

We didn't speak all the way back to Miss Ora's. I dropped her off in front of the house and watched her go up the sidewalk with an armload of clothes and a beat-up old suitcase. As irritated as I was, I smiled at her trying to make it look like it wasn't a struggle to get into the house without dropping something. Funny how something so insignificant can remind you how much you love someone.

And then there it was again, that fleeting thought that Mama would be so happy to see her coming up that walk. How many times did she pray for Gracie to come home? And here she is now – but Mama is gone.

My sister barely made it home in time for the funeral but did not see Mama before she died. We looked for her the entire two weeks Mama lay in a coma in the hospital; we kept her on life-support while we called everyone we thought might know where Grace was. Her ex-boyfriend-slash-pimp-slash-drug dealer had been in prison for several years with a rap sheet a mile long. It should have included sex trafficking, if you ask me. Gracie was only sixteen when she took off with him. He was twenty-eight, if my math is right. I went out to the prison to see if he might know where we should start looking for her. He refused to see me, which didn't surprise me at all.

I stopped in to see Eddie while I was at the prison. As a Public Defender, I'm out there a lot. I asked the warden to arrange for a private reception area and she did. Of course, a guard stood nearby. I hugged him tightly. He was so thin I could feel his bones through the scratchy wool sweater he wore over his orange prison-issued scrubs. He smiled up at me, his toothless grin as endearing as ever.

"You look good." I smiled and dropped my briefcase onto the table, pulling out two chairs so they faced each other.

"How's your mama doin'?" Those were the first words out of his mouth. I teared up immediately.

"Not good, Eddie," I removed my purse from my arm and hung it on the back of the chair. "She had a stroke a few days ago."

"No ma'am," Eddie said, a flat rebuttal.

"Miss Ora found her. She hasn't been awake since."

"No ma'am… No ma'am…" he repeated and dropped into one of the chairs.

He took his head in his hands and rocked it back and forth.

"We've been looking for Gracie, but we can't find her. The doctors want to take Mama off life-support…"

"She go'n die?" Eddie's head snapped up, his face streaked dark with tears.

I nodded and sat down at the table. I put my head down on my arms and wept for the first time since I called the ambulance to retrieve her from our little house on Rambo Street. We cried together. He kept saying he wanted to see her, and I told him they wouldn't let him go unless she was family.

"But she is fam'bly," he said. "She the onliest fam'bly I got here."

"I know, Eddie, but that doesn't count. I'm sorry," I said.

I wish I had known then that my mama actually *was* his daughter. It's hard to believe he didn't tell me himself. The lengths that man went to trying to protect us…

I did not return to the prison until after we buried Mama. I feel guilty about that now. At the time, I was tied up with grief and obligation. Shawn and Rochelle had always lived with her, and Grace was in no shape to care for them. I moved the kids in with me, and there were legal issues with everything.

I let Grace move into Mama's place and convinced her to go to rehab down at Lifeways, but she was clearly unfit to parent her children. Mama gave her so many chances to prove she could, but she always failed miserably. One of the times Grace came back home, Mama was so convinced she was clean that she took the kids out of daycare and let Grace keep them during the summer while she worked for Miss Ora. I stopped by one afternoon to drop off Rochelle's medicine from the pharmacy – she'd had an ear infection and the doctor called in a different antibiotic.

When I got to the house, Grace was sitting at the kitchen table with two people I didn't recognize. She swept the remnants of whatever they were doing up into her t-shirt and headed for the back of the house before it hit me what was going on. I asked where the kids were, because I didn't see them in the house. Mind you…Shawn was only seven and Rochelle just four, and all Grace could say was "They prob'ly down at the neighbor's house."

45

I didn't even give Mama an option that time. I enrolled them back at the daycare center and took it upon myself to make sure they were dropped off and picked up every single day. Grace was gone again shortly after. Mama said under her breath, "Idle hands the devil's work." That was one of her favorites. I got the impression she was blaming me for Grace's leaving, as if taking away her babysitting job left her with nothing to do.

Grace is still childlike in many ways. It's like she has never matured past sixteen, like she is a myopic teenager whose only concern is getting what she wants. She listens to no one. When she wants to do better, she does better. When she wants to use, she uses. I cannot change her, and I know this. All I can do is let it play out and try, try, try to limit the collateral damage.

13 – Grace

I got all my stuff put away in my room and it still didn't look like anybody lived in it. I had an armload of clothes that looked pitiful hanging in that big ol' empty closet. I went and found Miss Ora and asked her if I could go into Mr. Walter's room and find me something to read. She said she'd do me one better and take me to the library downtown. We decided to walk instead of taking a cab; it ain't but five or six blocks away. It was windy outside, but the sun was out, so it was plenty warm for just the first day of March.

I changed my clothes and met Miss Ora on the porch. She had a couple of canvas bags slung over one arm and her pocketbook under the other.

"Here, let me carry those," I said. "Looks like you tryin' to bring home the whole library or something."

She has a great laugh, Miss Ora does. Louder'n you might expect for somebody so tiny. I remember when I was little I would knock myself out to make her laugh, and she did. A lot. It was the first time I heard her laugh out loud in a long, long time.

"Well, I've done this before, Gracie-love." She the only one ever calls me that. "You remember when we used to pull that old wagon down to the library to bring books home for you? I never saw anybody read as much as you did. Wagon's gone. These bags'll have to do."

She right about that…always had my nose stuck in a book. Only way I could escape, I reckon. Truth is, I just love reading. When I was on the street, no matter what town I was in, I'd find the library first thing. I never had an address I could call my own, and sometimes none at all, so checkin' anything out was not an option.

With Miss Ora, I can get anything I want, though this ol' library is a little slow to keep up with the times. I like the big libraries like they got in Atlanta. I spent a lot of time there. That's where I was when Mama died. Easy to disappear.

I felt my chest get tight and I let out a long whistling breath. I could hear Mama as if she were right there with me. "Don't you be invisible, Grace Lowery. Don't hide your light under a basket. You let it shine, shine, shine." And then she would pull me tight to her chest, and I could smell bacon from that morning's breakfast and the sharp clean smell of Dove soap – the bar kind she always bathed with.

"Gracie?"

I shook the memory from my head when I realized Miss Ora was talking to me. "You all right?" I looked around to get my bearings. She was about twenty feet in front of me, looking back.

"I'm good," I forced a smile and walked toward her. "Just lost in thought, I guess."

"I was just talking away and realized you weren't beside me anymore. What were you thinking about?"

"I was thinkin' about – oh, a lot of things really. Mama mostly."

When I reached her, we moved forward together as if we'd never stopped.

"I miss her so much, Gracie. It feels like…it feels like…like one foot nailed to the floor most days. Like I don't know how to go through a day without her. I don't enjoy my routine without her in it. And not because of what she did for me. I can make my own breakfast and sweep the floor. Always could, and half the time did. It was her company that made me feel whole. And now I don't. I feel half. I feel like the smallest half, the leftover piece of pie that nobody touches because it's the last one."

It would be so easy to hate her for carrying on like that. Like she the only one lost Mama and feels left behind. But I don't hate her. I know exactly how she feels and it don't feel good. I slipped my hand into hers. It felt cold, but soft like coconut oil, like her skin might slide right off her bones if you just pulled it with your thumb. I gave her a little squeeze and started to pull away, but she held tight to my hand and kept walking.

"We're going to be okay, Gracie-love. I know we are."

14 – Patrice

I passed Grace and Miss Ora on the way to the courthouse for my three o'clock case, but I don't think they even saw me drive by. Miss Ora's arm was bent, her elbow tucked tight to her waist, and she held Gracie's hand in both of her own. Gracie was laughing at something, her head thrown back and her mouth open wide. This is when she is the most beautiful. I can almost forget the bad things when I remember how she was as a child. We all doted on her, but she was not spoiled, not even a little bit. She was funny and happy and curious about everything. And smart as a whip, that's what I remember.

My case went as expected, and my client was remanded to the Lake County Jail. When will these guys ever learn? You can't ghost your parole officer, then show up high for court. Doesn't matter how good I am at my job, I can't defend pure stupidity.

I stopped by the county clerk's office before I drove home. I had them pull all the reports they had on the death of Skipper Kornegay, including Eddie's arrest, his bond, and his plea deal. I read the crime scene report first. I wanted to read it before I got home, and I forced myself to focus on just the details of the report, without imagining my brother creating the scene they described.

On Sunday morning, November 28, 1976, members of the Mayville Police Department, dispatched by Skipper's father Ralph Kornegay, the Chief of Police at the time, found Skipper's body in a small clearing in the woods north of downtown Mayville. The report, written by Officer Horace Lindsey, states Chief Kornegay thought Skipper might have run away again, or was simply hiding at one of his friend's houses, so he hadn't been worried the first couple of days. I got the impression staying gone for days was not uncommon for the boy. On Sunday, after several calls from his friends, Kornegay finally became alarmed and instructed the officers on duty to be on the lookout for his son.

According to the report, Lindsey was the first to notice the body, partially covered by leaves. After securing the crime scene, Officer Lindsey called for backup from two specific officers and asked a third to go by Chief Kornegay's house and bring him to the location.

The section of the report that described the scene were the most difficult to read. I didn't need photos – and I didn't request them – to visualize his body. I imagined his long, straight, pure white hair, matted with blood and dirt and leaves, and his wiry arms and legs bent awkwardly in death. It was fall; the ground would be a blanket of leaves then. It would be a tough crime scene to investigate. It had rained for two days and finding hair on the body or among the leaves would be like the proverbial needle in a haystack.

There was no mention of a weapon, which makes me wonder what happened to the knife Marcus told Miss Ora he used—a switchblade owned by Skipper Kornegay. The more I thought about it, the more curious I became, so I made a mental note to ask the state's attorney what he knew about the case. Probably not much, since it was before his time.

I know Chief Kornegay died years ago, but I wondered what had become of Horace Lindsey and what light he might shed on the investigation. It's unusual that a man was allowed to confess to a crime he did not commit, without too many questions being asked.

I want to be prepared when Miss Ora and I visit the state's attorney's office about her case. Sounds so odd to say. *Miss Ora's case.* How in the world did we get here?

15 – Grace

Been a long time since I was in the Mayville Library. Wasn't even the same one as before. They built a new one down at the other end of town, so it was a good long walk for me and Miss Ora. We parted ways once we got inside, and I was glad. It took a while to figure out where to even go. They had several rows of low shelves off to the side by the front doors. A big sign said Special Collections and I figured I'd hit those first. I always liked to see what subjects the staff came up with...I should say what white people came up with, 'cause they usually the ones doing the comin' up with. Black History Month was still on the shelves. Convenient, if not terribly creative. I knew I could count on all the regulars. Baldwin, Walker, Hurston, Hughes, Morrison, McMillan, they all there. I've read everything they wrote. Most of 'em twice.

But they had a few I never heard of. This Danticat lady... *Breath, Eyes, Memory*, that's the name of the book, even if I can't remember her first name. That's some heavy stuff, there. I gotta take that one slow. And I got one by Octavia Butler that I'll give to Shawn if it's too much for me. He likes science fiction more than I do. He don't like to admit it, but he's a reader like his mama. And they had a copy of *In Search of Our Mothers Gardens*, and I thought maybe it was a good time to read that one again. It's mostly essays. I remember the one about her mama dying. I might not be ready for that one yet, but I'm gonna read it anyway. I picked a couple of my favorites for Rochelle from the YA section. If I'm being honest, they're just as much for me as for her.

I thought long and hard before I hit the checkout line. I figured whatever I got, Miss Ora'd get as much or more, and I'd be the one carryin' all of it home. I was right, too, but she didn't force them on me. I offered. I don't know what makes me feel so protective of Miss Ora. Maybe 'cause she's even more fragile than me, if that's possible. She tiny all over.

I used to sit beside her on the couch while she read books to me tucked all up under one arm, 'til I got too tall to tuck anymore. Mama never did much readin', 'cept for the Bible, and that wasn't out loud. Miss Ora was so good at it, she make all the people in the stories come alive.

51

When I was on the street, I used to go to the library, dope sick and broke, and I'd curl up in a chair with a book and pretend like I was in Miss Ora's house. It was easy, 'cause it was her voice I heard when I read to myself.

16 – Patrice

We are settling into our new existence as smoothly as possible. It has been two months since my grandfather died. Two months since I learned who he was and what he sacrificed for us. Two months since I learned my sister was raped as a child, and that my brother killed the boy who did it. Two months since I learned the web of lies which both bound my family together and tore us apart. There is a reason for the clichéd mantra "one day at a time." This is the only way to navigate a shift of this magnitude. Two months. Sixty days. One. At. A. Time.

My sister has spent most of this time at Miss Ora's house. I made some phone calls and found a psychologist who is willing to make house-calls, and we have begun the process, not just of rehabilitation for Grace, but counseling for all of us. Kamilah is a former school mate and sorority sister of mine, but our paths only briefly crossed at the university. She is patient and has a great deal of experience with drug addicts, and yet she is no-nonsense—doesn't let Grace, or any of us for that matter, off the hook. She is, like us, excited about the prospect of having a small residential facility—a halfway house of sorts, but that is only in the works now. We'll have to wait and see what happens with Miss Ora. The prosecutor is still reviewing the files and her confession to see what, if any, charges will be filed.

I would like to say we have made progress. In many ways, we have. Shawn and Rochelle are getting reacquainted with their mother, which is going as well as can be expected when you have been abandoned for as long as they were. I came home one day and Grace was helping Rochelle study for an English test. She was teaching her the phonics rules we learned back in the day, and Rochelle was absorbing them with uncharacteristic enthusiasm. Apparently, they teach memorization over phonics these days, which is crazy if you ask me. Easier to learn the rules first, then memorize the words that break them.

There is a lot to love about my baby sister. She was always very bright and excelled in her studies until she reached high school. Grace can be the sweetest, funniest creature when she is sober. It's clear she loves her children, but she relates to them as a peer, not a parent, and that is absolutely terrifying to me. The kids started riding the bus home to Miss Ora's house again, just like they did when my mother was alive, and like Grace and the twins did as children. We thought it would be a good way for Shawn and Rochelle to get to know Gracie again with the familiarity and oversight of Miss Ora, but I pick them up every day and take them back home with me.

Yesterday, Miss Ora had an appointment to meet with the state's attorney and I had promised to take her. I asked Grace if she wanted to come with us, but she declined. Said she was tired and not feeling well. I had the fleeting thought that it was not a good idea to leave her alone, but I ignored my gut. I need to learn to trust her.

The appointment was for 1:00 p.m., so we left at 11:00, allowing time to drive over to the county seat and still grab lunch downtown. It felt good to do something normal for a change. The lunch, I mean.

We arrived at Barrett Hammond's office fifteen minutes early, but they took us right in. I knew the state's attorney well enough to call him Barry, but I opted for a more formal approach under the circumstances.

"Mr. Hammond, thanks for seeing us." I shook his hand firmly and introduced Mrs. Beckworth.

He gave me a brief bemused expression but took the cue and settled into a more business-like posture. Barrett Hammond is distinguished and charming with ice blue eyes and prematurely gray hair which has gone almost straight to pure silver. The fact that he is terminally handsome and a resolute bachelor is the subject of discussion amongst all the county attorneys, male and female, and he appears to like it that way. It would be easy to imagine him running for a much bigger office one day. There's something about him that screams politician, though he rarely says anything political at all. I think that's what gives him away.

"What can I help you with today, Miss Lowery? Your message was a bit cryptic."

I laughed. "If by cryptic, you mean brief..." I said. "This one requires too much explanation for voice mail. And I'll tell you right off the bat, this is as unorthodox as they come. I've never heard of a case quite like this one."

"I'm even more intrigued." He leaned back in his leather chair and flexed a pencil with his thumbs.

"Do you remember the Kornegay murder in Mayville? Back in 1976. A teenage boy was stabbed to death."

"Vaguely," he said. "That was the police chief's son, right? I was almost out of law school in '76, but it was a big deal back then. I remember that. Some homeless guy confessed, if memory serves."

"That's the one. Skipper Kornegay was a classmate of mine. And the homeless guy spent twenty-five years in prison for a murder he didn't commit."

That got his attention. He put the pencil down, slid his chair closer to his desk and leaned toward us, his blue eyes fixed on me. "If you think he's innocent, file an appeal, Patrice."

"Too late. He's dead."

"So why are you here?"

"It's a long story." I reached out for Miss Ora's hand. It was soft and cold and trembling with emotion. "Are you sure about this, Miss Ora? Once I tell him, we can't go back."

I had warned her not to speak without my instruction.

"I'm absolutely positive, Patrice. I don't want to die with this on my conscience, and I can't live with it anymore either."

"Do I need to record this?" Barry asked. "You're making me nervous."

I shook my head. "There is a transcript of the story, and I'll leave it with you if I need to. Clara Jean Smallwood took it down. Nothing official, but professional, nonetheless."

"Is she still working?"

"She retired the same time Judge Odell did. She's a friend of the family."

"Your family?" he asked me, looking slightly incredulous.

"Our family," Miss Ora pointed one finger back and forth between herself and me. "Clara was a friend of *our* family."

"I'm sorry. I didn't mean to offend you, I was just clarifying."

I waved away the apology. "It's complicated. No worries."

"So," Barry said, "you want to tell me the rest of the story?"

I gave him the bare details. The rape of my sister at age six by the teenaged son of the police chief. The lies my mother told us all because the truth was far too dangerous to admit. Skipper's death at the hands of the brother I idolized. Eddie's arrest and subsequent incarceration.

Barry finally interrupted. "Where's your brother now?"

"My brother is dead, Mr. Hammond. He was killed in a car accident the day after the…the day after Skipper's death."

"I'm sorry..." He sighed and squinted at me like he was confused. "So why are you bringing this to me now?"

Miss Ora looked at me and I shrugged. Might as well get it all out.

"That's where I come in, Mr. Hammond." Her voice was a little shaky, but she spoke with the same confidence I had always known of her. "I have a bit of a confession to make."

"I'm all ears."

Miss Ora told Barry the entire story, with some details I hadn't known. Marcus had run into Skipper downtown and confronted him about Grace's rape. Skipper chased him into the woods brandishing a switchblade knife, but Marcus overpowered him, wrested the knife away and stabbed Skipper to death.

"He came to my house afterwards," Miss Ora went on. "His mama was my housekeeper and we'd had Thanksgiving dinner together that afternoon. Marcus was distraught and bleeding from lacerations to his head and hands. I cleaned him up best I could, closed the biggest wound on his scalp with butterflies I cut out of first aid tape, and got him out of town as fast as I could."

"Did you know he'd just killed someone at the time?"

"He confessed it all, Mr. Hammond. I knew what he did and why he did it. The boy attacked him first. I considered it self-defense."

"Then why didn't you call the police?" Barry was irritated, I could tell, but still interested in the story.

"I'm getting there, Mr. Hammond. Bear with me." Miss Ora coughed and cleared her throat and I stood to get her a cup of water from the cooler I knew was behind me.

"Marcus had a driver's license, but he did not own a car. I had a car, but no license. My husband's Ford LTD had been sitting unused in my garage since his death earlier that year. I had to convince Marcus to take it. I gave him a bill of sale and enough money to stay in a hotel for a couple of days, and Marcus headed north on I-75. Later that morning, a tractor-trailer slowed unexpectedly in his lane and, as far as anyone could tell, Marcus never took evasive action. There were no skid marks on the road; he didn't swerve at all. His car struck the back of the trailer with such force that the entire roof of the car was stripped off and the vehicle completely lodged beneath the trailer. They found his ID and the bill of sale in his wallet and notified our local police."

"And no one ever suspected him of killing the boy?" Barry asked again.

56

"Why would they?" Miss Ora asked. "Marcus was never on the radar. We didn't report the rape, so there was no connection at all to Skipper Kornegay."

Barrett blew out a long whistling breath and rubbed his forehead like it hurt, then turned to me. I handed Miss Ora a cup of water and sat back down. She took a sip right away and smiled gratefully.

"I'm curious about those wounds, Mrs. Beckworth. You bandaged his head. Wouldn't someone have noticed that?"

Miss Ora spoke slow, like she was talking to a dense child. "He died in Georgia, in a car accident."

"Still...no one put two and two together?" Barry pushed.

Miss Ora pushed back. "No one looked any further than Eddie, Mr. Hammond. He lived in the woods nearby and Ralph Kornegay made up his mind who did it the day they found his son's body."

I reached over and patted Miss Ora's hand, her cue to let me speak. I understood Barry's confusion. I'd asked all these questions myself at one point or another. I took a deep breath and said what I'd never had the courage to say before. "I don't know if you know much about the African American culture, but we're pretty specific about funerals...what we call home-goings. We have a viewing beforehand, and usually an open casket throughout the service. But in this case, none of us saw Marcus before we buried him. That was at the funeral director's insistence. There was simply not enough of his upper body left to reconstruct. So, even if they had thought of Marcus as a suspect, which they apparently did not, there really wasn't much evidence to be found."

"Ah, Patrice, that's tough. I'm sorry."

That's part of his charm, the way he empathizes even as he is digesting the details of a confession. He shook his head, I could almost see his wheels spinning. He stood and paced, stopped to straighten a plaque on the wall, then returned to sit on the edge of his desk near Miss Ora.

"So, let me get this straight, Mrs. Beckworth – you knew about the rape and didn't report it. And you knew about the boy's death and you didn't report that, either."

"That's correct," she said.

"And you covered for Marcus?"

"I did."

"Did it ever occur to you that this might be wrong?"

"I'm not an idiot, Mr. Hammond. It was a risk I was willing to take under the circumstances. And if there was any doubt in *my* mind, it was dispelled when I saw what Ralph Kornegay's men did to Eddie when they arrested him. Lord only knows what they'd have done to Marcus."

"Wow." Barry looked back at me. "This is a lot, Patrice. I need time to pull some case law and see if we have any guidelines." He stood and returned to his chair, pulled out a legal pad and flipped it onto the desk blotter. "I mean, at first thought, it's entirely possible that the statutes have run out on everything. I'm thinking maybe *accessory after* or tampering with evidence. I don't know where this would fall on the obligation to report a death, but that's a second- or third-degree felony depending on the circumstances. I guess I'll have to assign someone to cover this, but I've got to be careful even there."

"It's a mess," I agreed.

"I'm just..." he hesitated. "I'm trying to figure out why you're bringing this to me."

"Who else would I go to?"

He shrugged. "Good point."

"I mean, obviously, *I'm* not in trouble. It's just...I'm an attorney now. I feel a moral and ethical obligation to report what I know. Besides the fact that Miss Ora was determined to tell Grace's story."

"Grace is the sister who was raped?"

I nodded. "It messed her up. Truth is, she's not a very reliable or even sympathetic witness. She's been an addict for years. But she remembers most of what happened if it comes down to that."

Barry closed his eyes. "But the rapist is dead, and the brother who killed him is dead, and the man who served time for something I'm assuming he had *nothing* to do with is dead. And all I have is your say-so on all of it. Is there any evidence at all?

Miss Ora shook her head. I interrupted.

"I'm not convinced there's no evidence. I pulled the police report. I find no mention of the knife Marcus said he took away from Skipper. A switchblade. Seems odd the murder weapon isn't even mentioned. It may not mean anything, but it sort of stood out to me."

"We'll take a look at that." He made a note on his pad, then turned to Miss Ora. "So what do you want out of this, a clear conscience?"

"No, I want to clear his *name*," Miss Ora said.

"The homeless guy?"

Miss Ora glared at our state's attorney. "His name was Eldred Mims."

Barry froze for a brief second, then nodded. "He had another name, though, didn't he? The papers made a big deal of it."

"They called him the Pecan Man," I said. "But we called him Eddie."

"That's right. I do remember because we talked about the case in law school. Who confesses to murder, for crying out loud, let alone if you didn't do it? No evidence to speak of, and he just up and says 'Yep. Guilty.' I guess I find that the hardest to believe."

"You and me both," I said. "But that's not all. Turns out Eddie was my grandfather. And that is really the answer to your question. Who does that? A man who loves his family."

17 – Grace

I hadn't been alone since before Mr. Pecan died, and it felt strange. I made some sugar water for the hummingbird feeder in the backyard. I'd seen a scout buzz the lobelia and knew there'd be more to follow if I had the feeders ready. Miss Ora and I sit out there sometimes on the garden bench and watch them little things dive bomb each other, fightin' over what's plentiful and easy to share. I sat there for a minute, watching to see if they'd come, but I got antsy real fast. It ain't the same out here without Miss Ora. It ain't the same without Mr. Pecan, but he been gone for a long, long time.

I went inside and decided to make cookies like Mama used to make. I dug around the pantry for flour and sugar, but all I found was white sugar and self-rising flour and that would never do. Then I remembered she had Tupperware canisters up in the cabinet and I looked up there to see what she had. I found the all-purpose flour, and a collection of tea bags that looked like they'd been there since I was little. Then I found an old tin canister of baking powder behind the plastic ones and pulled it out. Who keeps baking powder 'til it's older than Jesus? It don't last a year, much less two decades. When I went to throw it out, though, something thumped the inside like it was one big lump. I opened up the canister to find a wad of hundred-dollar bills fat as a cucumber. I peeled one off and put the canister in the cupboard behind the spices. I felt guilty for a minute, but then I realized she probably don't even remember it's there, if she ever knew at all. I checked the clock and called an old friend of mine. I walked downtown to the drug store and bought a pack of gum and a tube of lipstick. I ain't had new lipstick in years, and the color looked perfect on me. I walked back home slow, and Kenny drove by about two blocks from Miss Ora's. He pulled over and I stuck my head in the passenger side and handed him two twenties. He gave me what I needed and pulled away smooth as silk. I palmed the baggie and slid it into my pocket.

It's just in case, I told myself. But I knew better.

18 – Patrice

We got home from Barry Hammond's office to find the kitchen a wreck. Grace was proud though, and she promised to have everything clean before supper, so I didn't say much. I couldn't imagine where she'd get money for drugs, so I willed myself to believe she was just lonely and bored.

Shawn and Rochelle arrived about twenty minutes after we did. They were excited about the cookies. I'm not a huge fan of sugar, so I just stayed out of the way. Miss Ora and I made tea together and sat out on the front porch while Grace and the kids hung out in the kitchen laughing and talking. I remember closing my eyes, savoring the moment. Maybe there *was* hope after all.

19 – Grace

My kids loved them cookies. I froze some of 'em just so's I could have 'em ready when they got home from school. It's like they cut on a switch or somethin', like we never been apart. They show me their homework every day now – even Shawn startin' to let me back in. Been a long time since I had so much fun with my babies.

I went through them first two bills pretty quick, but I was careful to slow down after that. I don't wanna get back to where I was with the dope. I just need a little to keep me going some days.

Even Kamilah says I'm doing better. Seems like it's easier to talk to her when I feel more like myself.

20 – Patrice

I couldn't get a read on where Barry Hammond meant to go with the information I gave him. I still had some questions of my own, so I decided to delve a little deeper into my initial investigation. I found a phone number for Horace Lindsey and called him from my office. He answered on the third ring. I introduced myself and asked him if he had time to answer some questions about an old case.

"Depends on which case." His voice was low and gravelly and punctuated with wheezy intakes of breath. A smoker, I thought. Heavy one.

My gut told me to play this one close to my chest, so I gave him details that weren't exactly true or false.

"Well, my client is Ora Lee Beckworth and the case involved my brother."

"I don't know that I can help you much. That don't ring any bells right off."

"I'd really appreciate your help. Your name's on one of the reports. It won't take long, I promise. I can come by your house, or I have an office downtown if you want to stop by there."

"How 'bout tomorrow after breakfast. I eat at the café ever' mornin', I can stop by right afterwards, long as you're there early enough."

"That'll be fine. I'll be here whenever you can make it."

I gave him the address and crossed my fingers.

I needn't have worried, though. The next morning, Mr. Lindsey strolled into my office dressed in a pair of black jeans and a western cut plaid shirt, both of them ironed with crisp pleats in the legs and arms. Something told me this was his version of dressed up. I was right about him being a smoker, but perhaps wrong about the mode of delivery. His clothes bore the woody scent of cigars, which was slightly more tolerable than the smell of old cigarette smoke. He was a good old boy, no doubt, but there was a hint of decency in his eyes. I felt almost immediately at ease, despite the circumstances.

His handshake was firm and two-handed and he called me "Little Lady" three times before I laughed and said, "I think being past the age of forty disqualifies me from that title, Mr. Lindsey."

He took it as a joke but stopped himself the next time he said it.

"So, which case did you say this was Lit...uh, Miss Lowery?"

"Well, it's an old one." I motioned for him to sit and slid into my own chair behind the desk.

"No wonder it didn't sound familiar. I'm gettin' forgetful in my old age. Remind me what it was about."

"It was the Kornegay murder, Mr. Lindsey." I held my breath while he thought.

"The Kornegay murder?"

"Skipper Kornegay," I said, thinking he just couldn't place it.

"I know his name. There was only one Kornegay murder. I thought you said this one had somethin' to do with your brother. That's what threw me. You said Miss Ora and your brother. They's only one case ever involved Miss Ora, and that's 'cause she took in the man that killed the Chief's son.

"Look, I don't want to cause you any trouble here. I just have some questions. We've gotten some recent information that points to Eldred Mims' innocence and I'm just looking into it. Unofficially at this point."

"Ain't nothin' about that old man innocent. He confessed plain as day."

"I know the case. I also know some facts you may not know. I won't keep you long. Just a couple of questions, okay?"

"Fire away."

"Like I said, there is some new evidence. . . I'm sorry. . . information, not evidence. Evidence is what I'm looking for here. There is some new information that points to a different..."

I took a deep breath. I was obviously not at my best here. I choked on the word "killer" before I even spoke it, flipped quickly in my head to "perpetrator" and still couldn't find a word that felt right to describe my brother. I should not be doing this. I'm too close.

"You okay, Ma'am?"

I looked up and Horace Lindsey was leaning forward, his elbows pointing outwards as he was poised to rise up out of the chair.

I shook my head to clear my thoughts and forced a smile.

"I'm fine. This is hard for me. Just bear with me a minute and I'll get it together, I promise."

He relaxed and waited. I made a mental note then. The mark of a good investigator – doesn't feel the need to fill a silence with his own voice. Just sits there and listens.

64

"Okay, let's try this again. I got some new info on the case and pulled the police report just to check a few things. Looks like you filed the initial report, so I came to you first."

He rubbed his jaw and thought for a moment. "Could be, but not likely. I was on scene first and found the boy's body, but I would have briefed the investigator and turned over my notes to him. Doubtful I'd have filed the report, though I may have signed it."

"Gotcha. Well, there was one thing I was curious about and I didn't see any mention of it in the report. I was told that Skipper Kornegay was killed with his own knife, a switchblade, but I don't see any mention of it in the report. Did you recover a knife at the scene?"

I waited for a moment, expecting him to answer, but he just sat there looking at his hands.

"Mr. Lindsey? Did you hear the question?"

"I heard. I'm just tryin' to figure out who woulda told you it was the boy's knife. It's been a lot of years and my memory ain't what it once was, but I don't remember anyone discussin' whose knife it was outside of law enforcement.

"Then you did recover the knife. Why wasn't it in the report?"

"It *was* in the report. I documented it, tagged it, and took pictures of it myself. I didn't know at the time it belonged to the Chief's son, but I was pretty sure it was the knife that done the damage. That boy was slap full of holes."

"Let me ask you this, then," I said. "When did you know it was Skipper's knife?"

He squirmed a little and the chair creaked under his weight.

"Chief Kornegay recognized it right off. He's the one gave it to the boy."

"Any idea why it wouldn't be in the report now?"

"Well, I got an idea, but I ain't gonna say what it is. That case is closed and oughta stay that way. Ain't gonna do nobody any good to dig up old bones."

I hesitated another minute before I revealed anything to the old man. I didn't want to cause him any trouble.

"Mr. Lindsey, I am one hundred percent certain that Eldred Mims did not kill Skipper Kornegay. And the reason I know this is because my brother is the one who did."

I watched a succession of emotional responses pass across Horace Lindsey's face. Confusion, doubt, horror, guilt, more doubt.

"Who is your brother? How is that possible?" he finally managed to ask.

"Marcus Lowery was his name. He died before you even found Skipper's body."

"So he helped the old man kill the boy?"

"I'm telling you...Eddie didn't do it at all. Marcus killed him all by himself."

"How do you know this? How do you know?" He looked and sounded almost frantic. There is more to this than I thought. I just don't know what.

"My brother confessed to Miss Ora that night. He died in a car accident the next day and no one ever suspected him at all."

"No wonder..." Mr. Lindsey stopped himself. "Why would the old man confess if he didn't have anything to do with it?"

"You know, I can only surmise it was to protect my family. The story is long, Mr. Lindsey, and I don't have all the answers. But I do know the truth."

"Why'd he kill the boy, then?"

"Marcus said it was self-defense – that Skipper attacked him and he fought back. I knew my brother and I know he would not have made the first move. It just wasn't who he was..."

"He cut that boy to shreds, Miss Lowery. Did you see the pictures I took?"

I nodded. "I did. Hard to look at. Hard to know my brother was capable of doing so much damage to another human being. There are extenuating circumstances that put it into perspective, though."

"Such as?" he asked.

"He raped my six-year-old sister."

"Sounds like your brother was a friggin' monster."

"Not my brother, Mr. Lindsey. Skipper Kornegay. He raped my sister not far from where he was killed. Not that day, but some months before. Marcus found this out the day Skipper was killed."

Mr. Lindsey leaned forward, locked both hands behind his neck, and stared downward. Without looking up he asked, "Did the Chief know?"

"Miss Ora says she told him."

"When?"

"Just before Eldred Mims confessed."

"Son of a bitch," Mr. Lindsey muttered at the floor.

66

Part 2 – May 2001

21 – Patrice

Miss Ora had a doctor's appointment yesterday and I had promised to take her. I'm worried about these spells she's having. I'm even more worried about Gracie. She's sleeping way too much, which could be depression like she says it is, but it could also mean much worse. I tried to get her to come with us but, as usual, she refused. Our appointment was for 11:30, and it ran late. Then they wanted an X-ray, which had to be done at the hospital, so Shawn and Rochelle made it home before we did. In the short time between when we left and the children got off the bus, Grace managed to connect with a dealer, get high, and start a cleaning frenzy. We found Shawn and Rochelle in the living room, looking shell-shocked and trying desperately to focus on their homework as Grace buzzed in and out between the pantry and the kitchen table.

"Oh, my," Miss Ora said, stopping in the middle of the living room to gape at the mess in her kitchen.

There were boxes and cans of food stacked across the tabletop, various seldom-used appliances on the chairs, and a bucket of brown soapy water on the counter.

"What's going on?" I asked Rochelle. I guess I assumed it would take a female perspective to make sense of the chaos.

"Um, she's cleaning?" Rochelle's eyes were wide and her body tense.

My sister had yet to acknowledge we had even come in. She spoke every now and then to herself, but not to us.

"How long has she been this way?"

This time Shawn answered. "Since before we got home, I guess. It looked like that when we walked in. She opened a can of baked beans and poured them into bowls. Cold. Told us to eat."

"Dammit," I said under my breath. "Y'all go get in the car. I'll be there in a minute. Take my keys."

"I'll walk them out," Miss Ora said. I just looked at her for a minute. Was she really going to leave me alone to deal with this? Apparently, yes.

I learned years ago that it is never a good idea to greet an intoxicated person with anger or authority. It just makes the entire situation worse.

I took a deep breath and went into the "Gracie mode" I'd learned years ago.

"Hey!" I said on her next trip in. I said it as if we had not already been standing there unnoticed for several minutes. "You've been busy."

"Oh, hey! I didn't see you come in," Grace swiped her forearm across her face. "I was just trying to get this pantry cleaned out. Miss Ora's gonna be so happy when she sees it. She likes things real clean you know, but Mama ain't been here for years. It's all dusty and half the boxes are out of date. I threw some stuff out she don't use, and I labeled her Tupperware with a magic marker so she'll know what's in 'em."

Grace never stopped moving as she spoke. She wrung out the dish towel and finished wiping down the now-empty shelves, then started taking cans back into the pantry. She selected alphabetically, which took some time.

"Can I help you?" I asked. "I'm afraid Miss Ora might freak out a little when she sees everything turned upside down."

"Oh, she won't be mad, Sister," Grace said. "I ain't thrown out anything valuable. I'm just making it so she can find things. It's depressing just sitting around all the time. She go'n love it, you watch. Hey, help me find all the beans and carrots. Those go next."

I hesitated a minute. "Why don't you go outside and work in the garden a little bit. I'll clean this mess up."

"It's not a mess, Sister," Grace protested. "It's all clean, look! I scrubbed everything, even this old toaster and I don't even think she uses a toaster. I oughta just throw that out, too."

"Grace," I lost the last bit of hold I had on my temper. "You can't just go into people's pantries and start throwing stuff away."

"If she doesn't *use* it, why *keep* it?"

"It's not yours to throw out, Grace," I said as she passed by me for the third time. I reached out and grabbed her upper arm. "Stop!"

She pulled away so hard she stumbled and almost fell.

"I think you need to sit down and tell me what you're on," I said.

She stopped dead still and glared at me. "I ain't *on* anything. I am *working* as hard as I can to do something nice for Miss Ora, and you're spoiling it, like you always do."

"What did you take?"

"I'm clean, Sister. I didn't take nothin'! Why you doin' this?"

"I could ask the same thing. Why? Why in God's name, when you have a beautiful roof over your head and people working hard to make sure you're okay? You tell me, Grace. Why?"

Her energy seemed to drain in one breath. She exhaled and sunk inward. "I just...I just needed to *feel* something, Sister. It's just crank, that's all. It ain't a big deal. I wanted to do something nice for Miss Ora. I wanted to thank her for all she been doin'."

I gritted my teeth and stared at her for a long moment. "This is not how you do it. It's not. How'd you get the money? Did you steal it from her?"

Her head snapped up and she glared at me. "I've never stolen anything in my life."

I rolled my eyes. It does no good to accuse an addict. They lie when the truth will do them better. The front door opened and Mrs. Beckworth stuck her head in.

"Everything okay?" she asked.

"Yes, ma'am," I said. "Gracie was just going to her room to lie down. I'll finish up in here."

When Grace had gone to her room, huffing and puffing and acting mortally wounded, Miss Ora and I stood for a moment and just looked at each other.

"I've never seen anything like that," she said.

"I have. Many times."

"Go on home. The kids look like they need you. I didn't know what to say to them."

"I can't leave you with this," I said. "It won't take me long."

"It won't take me long, either. And I'll get everything back in where I can find it."

Miss Ora picked up a stack of cereal and pasta boxes and headed for the pantry.

"I'll say this much for her," she called as she stacked boxes in their place, "she has this thing cleaner than it has been in years."

I waited for her to come back into the kitchen before speaking.

"I'm worried that she stole something to pay for the drugs she took. Can you check all your valuables and let me know?"

Miss Ora looked stricken then, but it only lasted a few seconds and she recovered.

"Well, I'll look, but I don't think Gracie would...of course she wouldn't. Of course not."

I looked at her without speaking. She sighed and sank into the nearest chair.

"I'll do a little inventory and take my irreplaceable things to the bank. Most of what I prize is sentimental, but..." She trailed off, her throat catching as if she were about to cry.

"I can take her home, Miss Ora. There's no reason for her to stay here when Mom's house is just sitting there."

"I won't hear of it," she said. "That child needs me more than ever. I'm not giving up on her again. No matter what."

"I'll call Kamilah in the morning," I said. "I think she should come talk to her. In the meantime, she'll be revved up for a bit longer and then she'll crash. She'll probably sleep for a good fifteen or sixteen hours, so don't be surprised. If she has more stashed, you'll figure it out pretty quickly. Let me know if that happens or if she gets out of line. I'll call Chip and get him to come scare her into compliance."

"So what do I do if things get out of control?" She looked terrified.

"Call 9-1-1. Then call me." I said. "Best thing to do right now, though, is to leave her be. Don't try to reason with her. If she insists on a conversation, just listen and nod. Don't argue. It's pointless and will likely push her into an agitated state. I think she may be a little embarrassed right now, so I'm betting she stays in her room. Watch her though. If she sneaks out, call me right away."

Miss Ora nodded and went back to work. I left her then and took the kids out for pizza. It seemed like the best way to distract them, and it worked. For the time being anyway.

71

22 – Grace

I woke up in the middle of the night, starving half to death. For a minute, I couldn't figure out where I was. The moonlight through the window was enough to illuminate the room. Miss Ora's room. Her house always smelled the same, so I might have known just as easily if I'd kept my eyes closed.

I tiptoed into the kitchen and raided the pantry first. It wasn't how I'd have done it, but all the stuff was back in place. She's not all that great about snacks, but I did find a jar of olives and a can of cashews. I took them to the kitchen table and got myself a plate from the cabinet. Then I hit the refrigerator and found leftover ham and a tray of sliced cheese. I ate my little feast at the table and washed it down with tap water. Nothin' ever tasted so good as a comedown meal, and I knew for sure I was coming down hard. I could barely finish eating. My arms felt like lead and I hurt all over. I dragged myself back to bed and lay there feeling like hell and praying I'd fall asleep soon.

23 – Patrice

Grace kept to herself until early evening the day after the pantry incident. Miss Ora said she knew she'd come out in the middle of the night and gotten something to eat because the evidence was left on the counter, but Grace was still in bed when Shawn and Rochelle came in from school that afternoon. As a matter of fact, she was still in bed when I stopped by to pick them up. I almost told them to just ride the bus home, but I thought better of it. Best not to change their routines every time their mother has a set-back.

Miss Ora looked exhausted, so I offered to make us all something for dinner and she immediately agreed. "I have hamburger thawed out and plenty of canned goods. Maybe we can just do a meatloaf or something?"

Shawn and Rochelle threw each other looks of disgust, which annoyed me a bit.

"Well, I could just open a can of baked beans for you, if meatloaf doesn't suit your fancy," I said, half-kidding.

They both looked horrified, so I backpedaled fast.

"Okay, that was not funny at all, was it? Do you want to talk about what happened with your...with Grace, yesterday?"

Rochelle shook her head.

"You got any peanut butter and jelly?" she asked, effectively changing the subject.

I looked at Miss Ora, who nodded at Rochelle. "I do. I have apricot preserves for you, and grape jelly for your brother."

"I'm not hungry," Shawn said and plopped into the chair at the kitchen table, his backpack sliding to the floor beside him.

"I find that very hard to believe," I replied. "You are perpetually hungry."

"Not today." Shawn dragged his notebook and science text from his backpack and got busy looking busy. I sat down beside him and motioned Rochelle into a chair as well.

"Kamilah is stopping by shortly to talk with both of you. I want you to eat something before she gets here."

"Why we gotta be here at all, Aunt Patrice? I mean, no offense, but I'd rather just go home after school." At fifteen, Shawn had just enough confidence to speak his mind, and just enough hormonal angst to stay quiet most of the time.

I sat and thought about that for a minute. I couldn't blame him, really.

"I know this is hard for you guys." What could I say that made sense? Hell, it didn't even make sense to me. "We're trying to get help for your mother –"

"Help her with what? Looks like she's got exactly what she wants right here." Shawn said.

Miss Ora chimed in then. "Don't be too hard on your mama. She's been through a lot."

"So have we," Shawn said, almost under his breath.

"Whoa now," I looked up from making sandwiches and caught Shawn's eye. "Don't be disrespectful."

"She just does weird stuff," he said. "And what do her problems have to do with us anyway? Aunt Patrice already said we aren't gonna be living with her anytime soon."

"Well, I know, but I think the goal is to get your mama well enough so she can take care of you again." Miss Ora said.

"Again?" Shawn shook his head. "She never took care of us to begin with."

"But you lived with her when you were younger. I remember a time when Grace stayed home with you. You remember that, right?" Miss Ora reached over and patted Rochelle on the hand.

Rochelle looked like a deer in headlights. "Uh-uh." She shook her head and glanced at her brother as if she were making sure it was the right answer.

"You want to know what we remember, Miss Ora?" Shawn sat up straight then. "What I remember is that Mama used to take us with her to a bar over on Pine Street. It had a screen-porch on the back of it and a little patch of grass in front of some dumpsters. She used to set us out there to play and make me watch Rochelle 'cause she wasn't old enough to know not to go out in the street. I 'member it was hot and stinky and we were always hungry, even though Gramma kept food at the house for us. And Mama made us swear not to tell Gramma. That's why 'Chelle's lookin' at me like that. She's *still* scared to talk about it."

"I ain't scared," Rochelle protested.

74

"Right," Shawn said. "And you weren't scared of that nasty ol' man used to make you sit on his lap either, were ya'?"

Rochelle tilted her head down and went mute.

I stepped in then. "Why haven't you ever told me this?"

"You haven't ever asked," Shawn snapped. "Ain't *nobody* ever asked."

"What was your mama doing while all this was happening?" Miss Ora was too horrified to realize she was treading on awfully shaky ground. I wished she would just be quiet.

"Sometimes she worked the bar," Shawn answered. "Sometimes she sat there and drank beer. And sometimes she disappeared long enough for ol' Raymond to start in on us...mostly 'Chelle, 'cause he knew I didn't like him none."

"Did you tell your mama he was bothering you?"

"Huh. Lotta good that did. She just laughed and said, 'Baby, ol' Raymond ain't go'n hurt you. He jus' like kids.'" His impression of her voice was remarkably accurate. "Then one day he brought a Nestle's Crunch bar for Rochelle and told her he'd give it to her if she sat on his lap, and she did. Mama got mad when she came back in."

"Well, thank God..." she said.

"Noooo – not at him," Shawn said. "He kept tickling her, even after she started cryin' and I bit him on the arm and pulled her down off his lap. She was pissed at me, not him."

"Did Blanche know all this?" Miss Ora asked.

"I have no idea what Gramma knew," Shawn said. "Mama made us keep quiet about everything."

I brought peanut butter sandwiches to the table and put Rochelle's in front of her. She did not take her eyes off her lap, nor acknowledge that I was even there.

"I think that's enough for now," I said to Miss Ora. "We need to wait for Kamilah to discuss these things."

"I don't even know why we have to talk about it at all, Aunt Patrice." Shawn packed up his homework and shoved it into his backpack.

"What are you saying, son?" Miss Ora asked.

"I'm saying, what's the point? What's the point of us coming here every day? So she can ignore us? So she can feed us cold beans from a can? Really – what's the point? I'd rather be home. And so would Rochelle. There ain't nothin' to do here. No Playstation, no movies.

75

Just homework and a crazy woman draggin' shit outta closets. She doesn't even *want* to be our mama, so what's – the – point?"

Shawn raised his voice with each word he emphasized, then slid his chair back hard and left the room. Rochelle just sat there looking embarrassed and confused. I wish Miss Ora would just butt out sometimes. Really, I do.

24 – Grace

When I finally woke up this afternoon, it was to the sound of people talking in the kitchen. I got up and put on some clothes and headed for the kitchen. I stopped when I realized Miss Ora was talking about me to my children. I stood in the hallway and listened. Coupla' times I started to go on in and stop it. I don't know why I didn't. It's hard to listen to things that ain't exactly true. Ain't exactly lies either, but whatever. Shawn remembers what he wants to remember, I guess...not that I blame him, but there *were* some good times, I swear there were.

Ol' Raymond never hurt my kids, I can tell you that. I'da killed him and he knew it. I don't know why Shawn's making such a big deal of that. It wasn't like we were there every day or anything. I just helped out sometimes 'cause I needed the money. And I could drink free. Mama didn't allow beer in the house anyway. She was like that. Anyway, it ain't as big a deal as he was makin' it out to be.

He came stormin' down the hallway after he said all that stuff to Miss Ora. I guess he was headed for the bathroom, but he was lookin' down and didn't see me until he 'bout ran into me. I caught him by the arms and held him there for a second.

"Baby," I said to him, but he wouldn't look up. "Look at Mama."

When he finally raised his eyes up at me, I said, "Why you say all those things to Miss Ora?"

He pulled one arm out of my grip. "Because they're true," he says, and pulls the other one away, too.

I watched him walk into the bathroom, then I turned around and walked back into my room and shut the door. I can't change his mind and I ain't gonna try. I just gotta do better, then he'll see. I do wanna be his mama. I just don't really know how yet.

25 – Patrice

Kamilah arrived around four-thirty. She seemed worried, but not surprised.

"It's part of the process," she said. "She's going to relapse. She's going to mess up. It's all about damage control at this point. Are the kids okay?"

I shrugged. "They're fine. Tired. Annoyed, maybe, but fine."

"How about you?" Kamilah leaned close and studied my face.

"The same."

"You don't look fine," she said. "You look pissed."

"Bingo." I pointed my finger at her for emphasis.

"You have every right to be; I would be, too. But it won't help anyone to show it."

I clinched my fists and willed myself not to scream. First of all, I'm an attorney. We are *trained* to hold our emotions in check, so she's preaching to the choir here. Secondly, I'm *human*. I am *not* a machine. I cannot keep holding and holding and holding while everyone else wreaks havoc around me. But I did not say these things to Kamilah. I just rolled my eyes and threw both hands up in the air. Seriously – what's the use?

"Let's go sit somewhere and talk." Kamilah took me by the arm and led me to the front porch. We sat in the rockers and rocked silently for a while. I stared out across the street and noticed my friend Cheryl's car at her mother's house. We'd lost touch over the past year or so, though we had been inseparable at one time. She'd married straight out of college and divorced four years and three kids later, much to Dovey Kincaid's horror. No Kincaid had ever divorced, though that was not so much the issue as the fact that Dovey had been openly critical of any of the town's divorcees over the years. I remember Mama muttering, "Well, ain't the chickens come home to roost." She liked Cheryl, though. I liked her, too, and I missed her company.

"Where are you?" Kamilah's soft, full voice interrupted my thoughts.

I smiled and closed my eyes for a moment. "Far, far away, I think. But still here."

"Tell me what happened." Kamilah slid the pen from the center of her binder and clicked the point into place.

"We had an appointment with the DA. When we got home, the kids were here and Gracie was high. Crank, she says, and I would have guessed that anyway. She was rearranging the pantry."

"Good guess," Kamilah gave a wry laugh.

"I'm so tired of this." I dropped my head and fought back tears. I don't even remember the last time I cried, and I did not want to start now.

"I don't know if this will help or not, but you're doing a really good job here, Patrice."

I know she meant well. I do. But that one statement just went all over me. I felt my entire body tense as I grabbed both arms of the rocking chair and rose up out of my seat. I stepped to the railing of the porch and braced myself, stiff-armed, against the flat top of the rail. I took in a ragged breath, then turned to face her.

"Honestly?" This came out like a shriek. A wave of surprise washed over her features, and I almost felt bad. Almost. I lowered my voice and plowed on.

"Of all the people in the world, I'm the very one who knows I'm doing a good job. I did a good job in high school and college," I said, pushing one index finger down with the other, then moving down the line as I spoke. "I did a good job taking care of my mother when she needed help, and my siblings while Mama worked. I've done a good job raising Shawn and Rochelle, and I've done a *great* job cleaning up all the messes my sister made, and I am sick of it. *Sick* to *death* of all of it. And all I get from you is 'it won't help to show it?' Really? What do y'all want from me, blood?"

Kamilah stood slowly, set her pen and writing pad down on her chair, then reached out and took my hand. "I'm sorry, Patrice." She pulled me toward her and wrapped me with both arms. My hands hung awkwardly until I surrendered, threw my arms around her waist and buried my face in her shoulder.

"You *have* done a good job, and you've mostly done it alone. But you aren't alone anymore. I have a plan. *We* have a plan, and it *will* work. I want you to hear me, Patrice. The plan will work if we work it."

I sobbed into her shoulder for several minutes. Her long braids pressed into my cheek and smelled like earth and sage and something else I couldn't place, but it felt powerful and true and I decided to trust her. When I relaxed and pulled away to wipe my eyes, she held me at arm's length and said, "You don't cry enough, do you?"

"What's enough?" I swiped at my nose with my sleeve.

She laughed. "Sit," she said. "Let's talk about the plan."

I sat. She talked.

"We used to believe addicts had to *want* to get better before we could treat them, and that's still partially true. Families are told to detach, to let the addict hit rock bottom so they'd have the motivation to seek help. But, I don't believe detachment means you have to stand back and watch helplessly while your loved-one self-destructs. And it certainly doesn't mean you have to face this problem alone. This is a *family* problem, not an individual one, which is why I was so excited when you asked me to provide counseling for your entire family. I suggest it all the time, but this was a first. A family already seeking help as a unit."

I shrugged. "That was Miss Ora's suggestion. I'm not gonna act like I was all gung ho on the thing."

"It won't work without you. Plain and simple. It will not work."

I'm sure I looked skeptical. I dropped my chin to my chest and let all my air drain out.

"Listen to me, Patrice. Like it or *not*, you have become the family matriarch. This family *revolves* around you...hold on. Hear me out."

I don't even think I noticed my head snap up when she said that. It took forcing myself to shut my mouth, which hung open in astonishment, to become aware of my reaction.

"I know, I know...you think it revolves around Grace. But let's step back a moment. It is the gravitational pull of the earth that holds the moon in place. You hold this family together, Patrice. Grace is the meteor shower that threatens your existence. We have no control over where those meteors go, but we can adjust our orbit to give them the opportunity to fall comfortably in line. Does that make sense?"

I scowled. "Not even a little."

"Alrighty, then," Kamilah laughed. "Let me come at it another way."

"I'm a concrete kind of person. Less metaphor, more specifics."

She nodded. "Got it."

I relaxed again as she went on. "Our plan is Structured Family Recovery, which requires everyone in the family to be on board with the program. You are the one person who could make or break it for everyone. I need you to understand and agree on the plan and help me implement it. I know it's a lot to ask, but I know it will work, and I know it will relieve *you* above all others in the end. What's done is done in this family. There is no therapy for what *should* have happened, only what *did*."

"Exactly!" I erupted. "And it happened to Grace. I didn't even *know* about it. Why is it my job to fix? Grace is the addict. Grace needs to fix it."

Kamilah nodded. "You're right. Grace is the addict. But listen to me, addiction *removes* her ability to exercise willpower and self-control. That's the nature of the disease. So let me ask you this: are you willing to put the responsibility of recovery on someone who has *no* self-control, no matter how much the family suffers in the process?"

I looked down at the dark green planks of the porch floor. A line of ants marched down the white pillar by the front stoop. At the base of the pillar, a group of them struggled to move the dead body of a wasp, which rocked back and forth at the effort.

"I'll do whatever you say," I said. "But I don't want to make *any* decisions for this family."

"Such as?" Kamilah picked up the pad and paper from her chair, then sat back down.

I leaned back on the porch railing again. "Like none. I don't want to decide when we'll get therapy or with whom. I don't want to decide anything about anything. You just tell me what to do and when to do it. Deal?"

"Deal," Kamilah said. "First assignment: suspend your anger at Grace."

I sighed. Heavily.

"This is just as much for you as it is for her. I want you to set a goal of a month. No matter what happens, don't react with anger toward her. We'll set boundaries and minimize opportunities for failure for Grace, but we can't control what she does, only how we react to it. So we are going to choose to act out of love and not anger, courage, not fear."

"If you say so," I groused.

"Honey," Kamilah said, "if I could teach this to you in one day, there would be no drug epidemic right now. You're gonna have to trust me. Love, not anger. Courage, not fear. Be brave, Grasshopper."

I laughed out loud then, and it felt good.

26 – Grace

Kamilah asked me about the rape today. Ain't nobody ever asked me about it before. Not even after they knew. Not Patrice, not Miss Ora, not even Aunt Tressa. I want to think it's 'cause they scared to upset me, but I gotta admit, sometimes it feels like they just don't care.

Kamilah cares. She easy to talk to. She don't judge me like everybody else. We were sittin' on the porch. Sister was in the kitchen makin' that meatloaf she promised, and the kids was parked in front of the TV while Miss Ora took a nap. She went up to her room about four o'clock and didn't come down 'til time for supper.

Anyway, Kamilah was real careful about askin'. "Do you remember what happened to you? Can you talk about it?"

I shrugged. "I ain't all that sure what I remember and what I dreamed. Mama was right, in a way. It was a bad dream I dreamed over and over and over, 'til I thought it would never go away."

"Has it? Gone away, I mean."

I had to think about that a minute. "I was just about to think it did, but I dreamt it night before last."

Kamilah nodded like that explained everything. "Can you tell me what you *think* happened to you? It's okay if you don't feel comfortable. Just tell me what you want to, and I won't push."

I ain't sure she needed to be so careful about it. I was glad to finally give this story a voice. I ain't ever been allowed to tell it before.

"I 'member feelin' proud 'cause Patrice let me walk to Miss Ora's house all by myself. I knew the way good enough, even the shortcut through the woods. We used to go almost every day when Mama got off work so we could walk her home. Miss Ora was always sendin' somethin' home with her – leftovers or magazines or bread that was gettin' old. She had a sweet tooth, so we were always gettin' cake and pie she couldn't eat all by herself. Even when Mr. Walter was alive, we'd get half of whatever Mama baked for 'em. Anyways, I know Marcus was at work that day, or I wouldn't have got to go by myself. Marcus said I wasn't old enough. But that day Patrice was on the phone... I don't know where the twins was, but Patrice was on the phone for a long time and I kept buggin' her to go show Mama the pictures I drew at school. Finally she just said, "Oh, just go then!" and I ran outta the house 'fore she could change her mind."

"How old were you?" Kamilah was leaning forward in her chair, her arms resting on her forearms. Her body almost looked folded in half.

"I was in first grade, so I was six, almost seven, I think. My birthday's in January."

"Young to be walking by yourself."

"Not back then. We had free run of the neighborhood and I'd walked to school with my friends since kindergarten. It's just what we did. But, yeah, maybe clear through downtown was a stretch."

"So, when did you…I mean, when did Skipper…"

"I took the shortcut through the woods. All the kids did. There was a bike path worn clear down to hard dirt. That white boy and three others were ridin' their bikes and 'bout ran over me comin' around the corner, but I heard 'em and stepped off the path. The other boys hollered and kept on goin' but that white-haired one hit his brakes and slid his back tire around so he ended up right beside me."

"Did you know the other boys?"

I shook my head. "I didn't know none of 'em. Anyway, this is where my memory gets weird. There are parts where my body remembers better than my head does. I remember him askin' where I was goin' and if I wanted a ride. I told 'im Miss Ora's house and he said he could take me there. But I don't remember if I got on the bike or not. Sometimes in my dreams, I did. Sometimes I said, "No, thank you, I can walk.

I remember bein' real polite like Mama always told me to be with white folk. And then…" I squeezed my eyes shut and tried to get a clear picture in my head. "I remember him bein' on top of me, and we weren't on the path anymore. I can't figure out what's missin'. I just remember fightin' and screamin', and then his hand over my mouth so I couldn't breathe, and him sayin' he was gonna cut my throat if I didn't shut up. And at some point two of the other boys came back, and I could hear 'em laughin' and sayin' 'Hurry up, hurry up,' and I guess I passed out, 'cause when I woke up, he had me pinned to the ground, layin' flat on top of me, and I screamed again…"

I stopped talking for a minute—I could see him clear as day laughin' like he'd done somethin' he was proud of, and tellin' me I better shut the hell up, and spittin' in my face. I could see it in my mind, but that's when I felt the panic risin' up in my chest and I knew I couldn't say the words to Kamilah. I opened my eyes and swiped at the tears spillin' down my face. "I don't know why I'm all the sudden emotional. I ain't cried about this for years." I looked at Kamilah like maybe she could explain it.

"Nothing wrong with crying," she said. "You can stop talking, or you can go on. You're doing great."

"I'm not doin' great at all." I held my shaky hands out for her to see. "I need a drink. I need somethin'. I feel like I'm gonna crawl out of my skin."

"It's okay. I'm going to sit with you through this." Kamilah pulled her chair around so we were sitting knee to knee. She looked toward the door and called for Patrice, then looked surprised. "Oh, you're there," she said.

I looked over my shoulder. Patrice was holding the door slightly open. I could tell she'd been crying.

"Do you need me?" she asked Kamilah.

"I was going to see if you'd get us some tea or coffee or something. Are you okay?"

"Yep," Patrice wiped both eyes with the heels of her hands. "I'll be right back."

"How long you reckon' she been standin' there?" I don't know why I asked when I was pretty sure I knew the answer.

Kamilah just sat staring at the door. Then she took both my hands in hers and just held them a minute. "Do you believe in prayer?" she asked.

I nodded. "You wanna pray?"

"I do, if that's okay."

"Can we wait for Sister?"

"Absolutely," Kamilah said, then smiled.

We sat quietly for a moment, until a commotion from the kitchen made us both leap from our chairs and go inside.

27 – Patrice

I shouldn't have eavesdropped, but I couldn't move. I'd come to tell them it was time for supper and when I opened the screen door, I heard Gracie say something about Marcus being at work that day. It seemed like a bad time to interrupt, so I stood there a second and tried to decide what to do. I could go tell Miss Ora and come back, but then Grace was talking about Marcus saying she was too young, and me letting her walk to Miss Ora's by herself.

When Kamilah looked up to call for me, I felt a jolt like a taser, electric hot, and my heart actually hurt in my chest. I tried to play it off like I'd just opened the door, but she had to know.

She asked me for tea, or coffee, or something. I stumbled back to the kitchen just in time to see Miss Ora coming down the stairs and I turned to face her.

"Patrice?" Her voice sounded like she was inside a tunnel. "Patrice!"

"I need to sit down," I said. Darkness started closing in through my peripheral vision and the next thing I knew, I was sitting on the couch with a cool washcloth on my forehead. Miss Ora was on the phone and Gracie was pacing. Kamilah was in the wing chair across from me making notes in her binder.

"She's okay," I heard Kamilah say to Miss Ora. "I don't think we need them."

Miss Ora covered one ear and walked into the kitchen with the phone still pressed to the other. Grace sat on the edge of the couch and took my hand in both of hers.

"Sister?" She leaned forward, her head bent over mine, eyes searching my face for something I couldn't quite place. Reassurance?

I know Grace is an adult now. I knew it was an adult sitting beside me, her frail fingers worrying my own. But I could only see Gracie the six-year-old, looking up, not down, asking over and over, "Sister, can I go? Sister, please? I know the way. Sister, can I?"

I felt the tears spill hot and reproving down my cheeks and neck. "I'm sorry, Gracie," I said. "I'm so sorry."

28 – Grace

I finished getting dinner ready, even though none of us felt much like eating. I could see Rochelle was worried. Shawn don't let on he's upset, he just his same teenage self, shuttin' all the rest of us out. Patrice invited Kamilah to stay, but she said she had to get on home.

I didn't know they knew each other in college. That came out when Kamilah asked if Patrice was going to the Alpha Kappa Alpha gathering in Gainesville next month. Apparently she and Patrice were sorority sisters. Kinda puts a new spin on things if you ask me, but I didn't say nothin'. We had enough cryin' for one day already.

When everyone was gone, me and Miss Ora got into our pajamas and robes and had decaf coffee together and pined after some a' Mama's good cakes and pies.

Miss Ora said, "I should have paid attention to what she did in my kitchen. She never wrote any of her recipes down. If I asked how she made something she said, oh just—"

"Summa this and summa that," I finished with her. "Re'Netta got the cookin' gene. Danita's pretty good, too. I got to where I don't care enough about food to cook it myself."

It felt good to just sit with Miss Ora. I don't tense up with her like I do with Patrice. When Miss Ora talks to me, she just talkin', and I can take what she says at face value. With Sister, I think what she says is always loaded with somethin' else. Makes it hard to know if I'm bein' set up or not.

"So how's it going with the prosecutor and all that?" I asked after a minute of peaceful silence.

Miss Ora looked surprised.

"It went as well as could be expected, I suppose. I think there are more questions than answers right now. The state attorney seems to think it may be hard to unravel, given the fact that most of the people who were impacted are dead now. Not many people left to testify."

"Except me." My voice felt small and insignificant, and I wasn't even sure I said it out loud, until Miss Ora put her hand on my arm and squeezed a bit.

"That's right, Gracie-love. Except you. And you're why I'm doing this. Because it matters to you."

I nodded and rubbed at my eyes. I was *not* going to cry in front of her.

"So," I forced some sound into my voice and spoke without really even thinking, "I'm not sure what all you're trying to do."

"Well, there are a few factors to consider, but the main thing I want to do is clear Eddie's name. I want the truth told, no matter what happens to me."

"And what do you think *will* happen? Will you go to jail?"

She took a long, deep breath before she answered. "I hope not, Grace. I'm old. I doubt they'll incarcerate me even if they do bring charges."

"What would they charge you with? I mean, if they was gonna charge you."

"You'll have to ask Patrice that question. I'm not a lawyer. I covered up a crime is what I did. I packed Marcus up knowing he'd killed that boy. I believed it was self-defense, but I knew it was a crime to destroy evidence. Worse, I let an innocent man go to jail for life and I never spoke up."

"I don't mean to hurt your feelings, Miss Ora, but I don't know how you could do that. Mr. Pecan didn't never hurt nobody. It makes me sad to think of him in jail all by hisself."

She just nodded and looked at her coffee cup, her hands wrapped round it like parentheses. We sat quiet for a minute or two. Then she said, "That's why I want to clear his name. It's the least I can do for him."

"What'll that do to Marcus's name then? He go'n be called a murderer now?"

"Not if I can help it. I told the story clear, just the way Marcus told me. Skipper admitted he raped you, and he laughed in Marcus's face. Then he pulled out a knife and tried to kill Marcus, but your brother was stronger. Hard to imagine someone hearing the story and not understanding, although…"

She stopped abruptly and wrinkled her forehead.

"Although what?"

"Nothing," she said. "It doesn't matter what anyone thinks. I know the story and I'm going to tell it until everyone believes me."

"Who don't believe you?" I demanded.

She fidgeted in her chair. "It's not that he doesn't believe me, Grace. He just wants to see some evidence and I don't have any."

"Evidence of what? They got the evidence in the files, don't they?"

"Well, yes... and no," she said. "He wants..."

"What? What does he want?" I was gettin' aggravated. She was hidin' something.

"He wants evidence you were raped—says all this is just hearsay and not proven and he doesn't understand why your mama never filed charges against Skipper. I tried to explain, but... I don't know. Some things just never change, I guess."

"I wanna talk to him. I'm the evidence. I'm the evidence, Miss Ora. You let me tell him."

"I wish it were that simple, Grace."

"You don't think he'll believe me."

I hate feeling hopeless. Hopeless sets on you like a stone and the more you try to crawl out from under it, the heavier it gets. I looked up at Miss Ora and all I saw on her face was pity, and that just set one more stone on top of the other.

"I'm sorry, Gracie..." she said. "We've got to get you healthy first."

I could feel my face pulling in on itself. Wasn't no way I was gonna avoid it. Some things never change is right. My word ain't never gonna be enough. I put my head down on the table and just let the tears come. Miss Ora let 'em come, too. She didn't tell me to stop, didn't say a word. She just sat and patted my arm 'til I was done.

And when I *was* done, it was like all that cryin' just loosed a flood of questions. I knew it was late and Miss Ora was tired, but I needed answers to all the things that didn't make sense. I raised my head off the table and took a sip of my cold coffee.

"So Patrice really didn't know."

"She did not. Your mother forbade me to speak of it in front of anyone."

"Why'd she do that?"

"We never discussed any of these details, Grace. If I had to guess, I'd bet she knew Patrice would never forgive herself for letting you walk here alone. She was determined to make you believe it simply never happened."

"I'm never gonna understand why she did that."

She paused then, stood up from the table, took our coffee cups into the kitchen and rinsed them out. When she came back to the table, she

88

pulled her chair closer to me and sat down. She always so proper, her back straight as a lamppost, only her hands resting on the table, never her elbows. She drilled that into me so much I notice it right away, even if the teaching didn't exactly stick with me.

"I've asked myself why a thousand times. And I asked your mama before she threatened to leave me if I ever asked again."

"Mama did that?"

"She certainly did, and she meant it. There was a lot I decided to risk over the years, but your mama's company was not one of them. I needed her, plain and simple. And she needed me, too. We were drawn together by more than this one secret, but it became both a magnet and a wedge as the years passed." Miss Ora hesitated again, like she wanted to say something else.

"What?" I prodded. "Just say it, Miss Ora."

"The last thing in the world I want to do is dishonor your mother's memory. I feel a tremendous responsibility to tell the story right, to not misrepresent what she did, nor to speak for her when I'm not certain her intent. But I can tell you this: your mama was devastated by what happened to you. I came home from the grocery store and she was there in the living room, holding you in her arms and weeping. I begged her to call the police, but she would not do it. She was determined not to put you through more trauma, and that's what she believed it would be. Not justice. Not care. Not compassion. Just more trauma."

"Is that what you thought it'd be?"

Miss Ora got this kinda vacant stare on her face and started tearing tiny pieces from a coffee stained napkin. Her fingers was shakin' like she was cold.

"I had no concept of being treated badly because of who I am, so I don't have an answer for that question. But what I do know...what I saw in her face and heard in her voice was palpable fear. And your mama was not a fearful woman."

"You right about that." I laughed a little when I said this, and for a second, Miss Ora laughed, too, but then she got serious again.

"Blanche was strong in everything she did, including standing up to me. There was always a battle of wills in this kitchen, and I lost just as often as I won. She kept me on my toes, and I liked that about her." Miss Ora dropped the napkin she was butchering and laid both palms down on the table. "Here's the thing, Grace. I didn't believe you'd be treated badly if we called the police. It didn't make sense to me at all. But, I

89

knew *she* believed you would, and I had to defer to her. I had to, but..." She slapped the table and her bracelets jangled.

"But what?" I asked.

"But, I hate that it was so easy to let it go. If I'm honest, I remember feeling relieved almost. That's a horrible thing to admit, isn't it?"

I didn't have an answer for that.

"I *wanted* justice for you, Grace. I did. I knew Skipper Kornegay. I saw him around town and, every time, I just wanted to kill that little bastard myself."

It wasn't funny, but I laughed anyway. I ain't never heard Miss Ora curse, and it just flowed outta her mouth slick as butter.

"Well, I *did*," she said. "Bottom line is, your mama didn't believe there'd be any justice served, not with Skipper's daddy being the police chief. Not with you being..." She stopped herself from finishing that sentence, so I finished it for her.

"A black child accusing a white boy."

"Exactly."

"So why'd she tell me it was a dream? Why didn't she just tell me the truth?"

"I don't know. Maybe she thought it'd be easier to forget. I think she just wanted it to go away, but it never goes away, does it?"

"No ma'am, it don't."

Miss Ora gave a little whoop and clapped her hand over her chest.

"You okay?" I stood up and leaned toward her, but she waved me away.

"Flutters. They happen all the time now. Takes my breath away every once in a while."

"You ask the doctor about that yesterday?"

She don't take care of herself like she should. Too busy worryin' about everybody else's business if you ask me.

"I did. He says it's generally harmless, but he gave me a new medication to take."

"You takin' it?" I'm onto her and she knows it.

"Yes, Miss Nosy, I'm taking it." She sounded snappish, but she was smiling when she said it. She likes it when you worry over her, even if she pretends not to. Mama used to laugh about that all the time.

"One more question..." I began after we both got quiet a minute.

"Go easy on me. I'm feeling a little weary."

90

"I remember waking up in your bed after… after it happened, and Mama tellin' me I had a bad dream. But I don't remember how I got here, and it gets a little confusing in my head 'cause I can't remember which part actually was a dream. Does that make sense?"

"Eddie walked you here. He heard you crying and found you in the woods."

"Mr. Pecan did?"

She nodded. "Yep. Delivered you to your mama's arms."

"What I can't figure out is, if waking up in your bed is part of the dream, or if I really did wake up here."

"You woke up here, Grace. It never was a dream."

I get so frustrated trying to sort this out. Even worse trying to explain it.

"Okay, I know that, but I started having nightmares right after the real thing happened, so I'm never sure. I took a bath in your bathtub and you brought me new clothes. Is that a dream?"

"No, that's real. I walked to Penney's to buy you an outfit because your clothes were…"

She clapped her hand over her mouth and her eyes got wide as the buttons on my bathrobe.

"What? What is it?"

"I have proof, Gracie."

"Proof of what?"

"Proof you were raped." She stood and left the room, heading down the hall toward Mr. Walter's old room. When she returned, she had a paper bag clutched to her chest. She picked up the phone and started dialing.

29 – Patrice

I had barely unwound from a stressful day when Miss Ora called me saying something about Grace's clothes. I couldn't figure out what she was talking about and I was *not* in the mood for more drama.

When I brought the kids home, I tried to explain to them what happened without oversharing - why I'd been so upset, how awful I felt, and how we are trying to get their mother the help she needs. But some things are just too much for them to know. I signed their homework for the next day and herded them toward bed. Shawn was happy to go. He cannot stand over-stimulation and, since his mother has returned, it seems like he's had stimuli on steroids. And now I'm adding to it.

Rochelle was full of questions and, quite frankly, I'm still processing half of it myself, so it's kind of hard to answer anything with confidence. With every new revelation there is some aspect of consideration required. How does this change what I thought I knew? What part did I play in this? Up until today, I thought I'd had very little role in what happened to Grace. Hell, I'm still not even clear what *did* happen. I haven't read Miss Ora's confession, yet, though I will now. But when will I have time? I've got work and children and Miss Ora's situation and counseling and Grace. Always Grace.

It's my fault. I was on the phone with a boy I had no business talking to in the first place. Mama would have killed me if she knew. He was way too old, and Miss Ora was right about him. She tried to warn me, but I thought I knew better. He had an agenda and as soon as it was accomplished, he disappeared.

I remember the day I let her go. She would *not* leave me alone. If I hadn't been on the phone, I'd have walked her over myself. That was the day Mama didn't come home. They stayed the night at Miss Ora's, which I thought was unusual and I was worried, but I never thought... I never imagined anything so awful. And now it plays over and over in my head. That's when Grace started acting weird. That's what I called it. Acting weird. She got quiet. Not at all the happy, chatty little sister I'd always had. Oh, that part came back eventually, but for a while, she just wasn't herself. When she hit her teens, it went downhill fast. I didn't even see it coming. I graduated from law school and came home to an entirely different sister – sullen, smart-mouthed and mean. That's what I thought.

And all these years of being angry, blaming Mama and blaming Grace, and it was my fault all along. The ringing of the phone jarred me from my self-recrimination.

Miss Ora didn't even bother to identify herself. "I have something I want to take to the state attorney."

"Okay," I mumbled. "What is it?"

"Gracie's clothes. The ones she was wearing when she was raped. They've been in a bag in Walter's closet. I thought maybe Blanche had taken them…somehow in my mind she had, but then I remembered. They were hidden in a hatbox. I have them."

She was breathless and her voice shook more than I'd ever noticed before.

"And why do we need those?" I asked. Maybe I was a little slow on my feet, but I blame the fog I was in.

"DNA, Patrice." She sounded annoyed.

"Uh, you do realize, Miss Ora, that if we turn that over to them, it is evidence of your obstruction. I think we need to think about this before we rush into anything."

"Well, of *course* it's evidence of my obstruction. What do you think I'm confessing to?"

I put the heel of my hand against my forehead and pressed hard. I was too tired to think. Too tired to make decisions. Too tired.

"I'll stop by tomorrow and we can talk about this. I want to call Aunt Tressa before we do anything."

"I thought you'd be excited."

"I'm too close to this, Miss Ora. We may need to get another attorney involved. I want to ask her what she thinks about that."

"Look, I've been clear, Patrice. I want this over with. I want everything out in the open, so I don't have to lie anymore. The stress is killing me. I'd rather go to jail tomorrow than worry and wonder if and when I'll be prosecuted. It's too much."

I took a deep breath before I blasted her. It should have calmed me, but I'm pretty sure it just brought oxygen to the flame.

"Have you ever once," I asked, slapping my thigh in frustration, "stopped to consider what anyone else wants or needs? You think *you* have too much to handle? I think maybe my mama spoiled you rotten,

Miss Ora. Either that or the privilege you have always taken for granted has simply blinded you to the very real possibility that the world is not at your beck and call. The world is not, and neither am I."

There was a deathly silence on the line.

"I'm sorry, Miss Ora, but if you want to take those clothes to the D.A.'s office, you can call a cab. I'll be in court tomorrow."

I felt awful. I knew I would feel worse in the morning. But I hung up the phone without waiting for her to reply.

30 – Grace

I don't know what Sister said to upset Miss Ora like that. She went back down the hallway and put that bag right back in Mr. Walter's room. Then she turned back around and went upstairs without saying a word.

I hit the redial button on the phone and Patrice picked up after four or five rings. She didn't even say hello, just started right in talking.

"I'm sorry, Miss Ora, but I just can't deal with this—"

"Sister, it's me," I said.

I heard a big sigh on the other end of the line and then her tight voice saying, "What do you need, Grace?" Like all I called for was to ask for something. Like all I ever did was need things from her.

"I don't need nothin', Sister." My voice was so cold and hard, it didn't even sound like me.

"Then why'd you call?"

"I wanted to talk to my sister. You remember her, don't you? The one that was so sad 'cause she thought she hurt me? That one. I called to talk to that one."

Another sigh. "That one's tired, Grace. I *am* sorry I hurt you. But to be honest, knowing what I did only makes it worse for me. I wish I could make you understand…"

"Understand what?"

"That it's a lot. It's a real *lot* and I don't think you get that."

"Don't be talkin' 'bout what I don't get, Sister. You ain't got any idea. How 'bout askin' yourself if you want to change places with me. 'Cause I'd trade with you today and I wouldn't be complainin'."

I heard her say something muffled, like she had her hand over the phone, then her voice got clear again.

"I'm going to hang up now, before I get mad. *Before* I say things that make you forget how much I love you. Because I do. I love you, Grace, and I love your kids. But they are *your* kids, not mine. They need their mama."

"I'm right here. I'll take 'em anytime."

"They need their mama *whole* and *sober* and ready to raise them. And let me just say this, Gracie. If I *could* trade with you, I would. I hate what happened to you, but I would take it on in a heartbeat if I could make

95

this family okay again. But what I won't do…and I want you to listen to me, because I mean this…what I won't do is be your punching bag."

I had to think about that a second, and by the time I opened my mouth to speak, I heard my sister say, "Goodnight, Grace. I'll see you in a couple of days."

31 – Patrice

I have to admit I was a little surprised I didn't hear from Miss Ora or Grace for the next few days. I wouldn't have put it past either of them to call me and act like nothing even happened, but my phone was silent.

So, instead of appreciating this time to myself, I found myself feeling envious of Cheryl Kincaid. She's divorced, for crying out loud – a single parent, but all I could think was, well at least she's had a life. All I've ever done is go to school and take care of someone else's kids. First my siblings and now my niece and nephew. I'm forty-one years old and I've never even had a real boyfriend, much less my own child.

I made an appointment with Kamilah and went to her office. I wanted to work through two things with her: first the noise in my head that counteracted the peace of their silence, and second, the seemingly impossible edict of suspending my anger. I'm still mad. Even though I've added a layer of personal responsibility for Grace being raped, I still find her absolutely infuriating. Impossible. Unreasonable. I've spent years, literally years, cleaning up the messes she makes. It's exhausting.

So why was it so hard to just step back and breathe? Kamilah was brutally honest with her response.

"Look, Patrice, either you do or you don't. Either you will or you won't. You set reasonable boundaries for yourself. You were clear enough about them. They obviously got the message. Either you are going to enjoy the respite, or you are going to obsess about details over which you have no control. And there's the rub, isn't it?"

I all but glared at her. "That doesn't feel fair to me. It sounds like you're saying I have control issues."

Kamilah shook her head and shot me a wry smile. "I'm not accusing you of anything. I'm asking, though I could have phrased it better."

"Then I don't understand what you're asking." I found myself feeling like a petulant child, which does not feel good. Not good at all.

"Sure you do. Are you going to use this opportunity to regroup, recuperate, *relax* a bit? Or are you going to spend your time analyzing their response to the absolutely reasonable frustration you expressed? You asked them to back off and give you space. They did. So talk it out a second. I don't want to put words in your mouth."

I felt a bit of explosion hovering just north of my lungs, and I breathed it back down. "I guess it's just that it's so out of character for them. Normally, they both try to placate me. Either that or they pretend nothing happened and we go on like before."

"Do you want to go on like before?"

"No. I don't."

"Change is hard. You said what you said, and they got the message. That's a step forward, regardless of how it feels."

"So I shouldn't feel like their silence is punitive?"

"You could do that. And it could well be. Then again, you could just make a generous assumption and decide that they are honoring your need for space and rest and trying not to overwhelm you further. Is that possible?"

"That they are trying not to overwhelm me?"

"Yes. Also that you can make that generous assumption. Are those things possible?"

I leaned back in my chair. "Yes. Both things are possible."

"So what will you do now?" Kamilah asked.

"I will enjoy the peace while I have it, and I will stop trying to control how they react."

Kamilah smiled broadly. "Beautiful. Now, do me a favor and take a deep breath and slowly let it out."

We did this together several times.

"How does that feel?" she asked.

I paused for a moment and focused on how I felt, not just emotionally, but physically. I twisted my head side to side, paying attention to how my skull rested on my spine, and the fluidity of the movement. I felt a sensation of lifting, of releasing a physical burden from my body, and then a gentle relaxation. I had the fleeting thought that I couldn't remember the last time I had done anything so intentional, but then I just sat with the ease that had settled over me and enjoyed it.

32 – Grace

Things were tense the next couple days. Patrice never called over the weekend, and Miss Ora kinda kept to herself. I dug through all my stuff and found a little something to ease my nerves. I'm doin' my best to stay offa the hard stuff, but I keep a reserve just in case. I don't wanna be back on the street, I know that much. I just don't think anybody really understands how hard it is sometimes. You can say all day long, I'm done. I'm *done.* But you're not done with the dope 'til the dope's done with you.

On Monday, the kids didn't show up after school. I thought about callin' Sister then, but I knew she was tryin' to make a point and would be waitin' for me to call. I didn't want to give her that satisfaction.

Miss Ora was worried though. I was out in the garage readin' a book and she came to find me about four o'clock.

"Have you heard from Patrice yet?"

I looked up when I heard her voice. She was still in a housedress, which wasn't really like her. She'll come down for breakfast in them sometimes, and she'll stay in one all day if she ain't feelin' well, but usually, she up and dressed for real pretty early.

"She ain't said boo to me, Miss Ora. I don't know what's gotten into her lately."

"Shawn and Rochelle should be here by now."

"I don't think they're comin'. Patrice wants to make sure we know she mean business."

She nodded and looked around the garage.

"I haven't been out here in ages. You have it looking like Eddie always did."

"This 'bout the only place I can get a good picture of him. I close my eyes and see him bent over this old chair, polishin' this, cleanin' that. He loved this old thing. Did you know he had a stash out here?"

"A stash of what?" Miss Ora looked horrified, which made me laugh. I couldn't help it. Her face – good Lord, her face.

"Don't worry, it was jus' Old Crow." She winced, which made me laugh harder. Maybe she'da been less offended if it'd been Crown Royal, I don't know. I slid out of the chair and bent down behind it. "He tacked a little sleeve under here. There was a pint bottle slid into it. Unopened."

She just gave a little shake of her head and said, "Oh, Eddie." Then her eyes narrowed, and she dropped her chin down and looked at me over the top of her glasses. "What did you do with the bottle?"

"Oh, I kept the bottle." I could hardly keep a straight face, and the look I gave her was half-daring her to ask about the contents, but she didn't. She just covered her face with both hands and rubbed her eyes underneath her glasses.

Finally, she just looked at me and said, "Well, it's a fine old chair, isn't it? I think we should see if we can find a spot for it inside the house, don't you? Shame to see it wasting away out here."

You can't get too far ahead of Miss Ora. She may be old, but she ain't stupid.

"I 'member when Mr. Pecan brought this old chair home. I spent hours helpin' him polish the scrollwork on the base. Makes me kinda feel like he's still here, sittin' up in this thing."

"It's a bit of a throne, isn't it?"

I patted the arm of the chair. "I need to get me a tiara, don't I? I can be the next Princess Grace."

I don't know why that struck us both so funny, but we laughed and laughed. When Miss Ora caught her breath, she said, "Oooo, I needed that laugh, Gracie, but now I need the ladies' room. You coming in?"

"In a minute," I picked up my book from the seat of the chair. "I wanna finish this one chapter."

Miss Ora started to walk away, then turned back toward me.

"Kamilah usually comes around four-thirty. You reckon Patrice has cancelled that, too?"

"Nah," I said. "She'll come around. She always do."

"What do you think of her? Kamilah, I mean."

I straddled the footrest and pulled myself back up into the chair. I laid the book back in my lap.

"Well..." I said, taking a deep breath through my nose as a way of stalling. I didn't really know if I wanted to answer that question, but then I remembered what I just thought about her. She probably already *knows* the answer, so I might just as well say what I think.

"You don't have to answer if you don't want," she said.

See what I mean?

"I was just thinkin' it over is all," I said. "Kamilah's good. She knows how to make you come at things like it was your idea. They do that a lot in rehab. I been in 'em enough to figure that out. They know you done had ten people tellin' you what you oughta do. Get a job, go to school, stop hangin' out with this guy or that guy. Fix yourself up, stop stayin' out all night, get up and get dressed. Why don't you take care of yourself? Why don't you take care of your kids? Everybody has an answer for your problems, 'cept they the ones denyin' what your problem really is. My problem ain't never been that I don't have a job. It's that they don't make enough drugs to kill the pain I'm in."

Miss Ora lip started to tremble a little. That's how I knew I said too much. I don't like when people get upset.

"How can we help you heal, Gracie?"

"Now, Miss Ora, you know what Mama used to say – you can't ask a fat man how to lose weight. If I knew the answer to that, I wouldn't be sick, now would I?" I jumped back up from the chair and gave her a little hug. "Come on, let's go in and see what we got to cook tonight."

***

Kamilah showed up just as me and Miss Ora was about to start supper. Patrice pulled in right behind her, like she'd been following her all along. The kids were not with her, which actually kinda scared me. What if something had happened to them getting off the bus and we didn't call to check? But she read my mind, I guess.

"The kids are at my house," she said. "I picked them up from school today. Kamilah thought it would be better to leave them out of this one."

"Scared me for a minute." I pulled at my collar to fan myself as I felt the heat rising to my face. I started to get mad, but then...I don't know...I was just so happy to see Sister, I hugged her and told her I loved her. She hugged me back, but I didn't exactly feel the love.

The four of us sat in the living room this time, instead of each of us talking to Kamilah alone. She was the one who suggested it. I gotta admit, I thought it was a bad idea.

Kamilah began with, "Patrice and I met earlier today, so I know that you hit a little rough patch last Friday. I feel like this is the perfect setting to discuss that and see if we can all get on the same page here. Does anyone have anything to say before I start?"

Patrice and I looked at each other, and I swear she had to be thinking the same thing I was: *I ain't touching this with a ten-foot pole.*

Miss Ora jumped in right away though. "I just think I owe Patrice an apology is all. I don't mean to be a burden, but I can see that I am." She said all this to Kamilah, then turned to Patrice. "I am so sorry, Patrice. I don't know what I was thinking. Of course you're overwhelmed. And I'm being completely thoughtless and expecting way too much from you. I just...when I found Grace's clothes, I was so excited, I didn't even stop to think what your schedule would be like. I just knew you'd be as excited as I am and that's not a fair assumption at all. Please forgive me. You've been so good to us and taken on far more than anyone should have to do. I don't know what we would do without you..." She got choked up then and stopped talking.

I could see Patrice felt bad then. She sort of fidgeted in her seat and her head dropped a little. "It's okay, Miss Ora. I know you don't mean any—"

"Hold on, Patrice." Kamilah held up one hand toward my sister.

"I'm sorry," Patrice said.

"Nope," Kamilah shook her head. "No need to be sorry. This is actually perfect. I want to ask you something. You just said, 'It's okay, Miss Ora.' But is it really okay with you what she did? And is it okay what she just *said* about what she did?"

"I don't understand," Patrice had a kind of deer-in-the-headlights look. "Am I okay that she just apologized? Is that what you're asking?"

"*Did* she just apologize?" Kamilah asked. "Because I think if you play that back, you might notice that she did more explaining than apologizing."

I didn't know where she was going with all that, but I started feelin' a little protective of Miss Ora. Patrice frowned and shoved her bottom lip out like she was thinkin' about what Kamilah asked."

"I don't know what to say," Patrice said.

"Look...this is going to be hard for all of you to hear, but I wanted you to hear it together so you'll understand what part *you* play in the dynamic between you all. So, Patrice, stop a minute and think what you were feeling as she was speaking. When you said, 'It's okay, Miss Ora,' what were you feeling?"

Patrice sort of slumped back in her chair and threw one arm across her eyes.

Kamilah leaned forward and put one hand on her other arm. "It's okay, Patrice. There's no right or wrong answer. Let me ask you this...when she said she was so excited about finding Grace's clothes and she thought you would be, too, what did you *feel*? Just give it one word."

"I felt bad," Patrice said from behind her arm.

I kept looking back and forth between Miss Ora and Patrice. I ain't even sure who I felt worse for. Miss Ora look like she jus' lost her best friend. Kamilah didn't even look at Miss Ora though. She was focused right on Patrice.

"When she said she didn't know what they'd do without you, what did you feel? One word."

Patrice sighed. "Obligated."

"And when she started crying?"

Patrice dropped her arm and sat up. She turned her head slowly toward Kamilah, like a light was dawnin' in her eyes. "Guilty. I felt guilty."

"And is that what an apology is supposed to make you feel?" Kamilah pressed.

"No," Patrice sounded plain indignant then. "No, it is not supposed to make me feel bad."

"Exactly," Kamilah said to Patrice, then turned to look around the room at each of us. "Today we are going to talk about co-dependency and enabling, and all the forms they take and behavior they inspire: manipulation, denial, guilt, caretaking, just to name a few."

I thought I was gonna have to get Miss Ora a bag to breathe in. "But, I didn't...I wasn't..."

"Of *course* you meant no harm, Mrs. Beckworth. Listen to me a minute. I'm not calling you a bad person, and neither is Patrice. No one sets out to be co-dependent, any more than they set out to be addicted. And co-dependency doesn't need the element of addiction to thrive in a relationship. What we are trying to accomplish here is a strong family relationship, right? Isn't what we all want for each other a healthy, happy, productive life?"

We all nodded, but nobody said a word.

"So let's look at where this family is co-dependent. Let's address the behaviors and see if we can get them straightened out. *Before* we even talk about substance abuse. Because that's just a symptom of the real problem, which I believe is an incredibly unhealthy co-dependency. But you know what? That's the easy part. If everyone knows what role they are playing, we can rewrite the script and get a better outcome."

We talked for two hours. I ain't felt that tired after anything, ever, not even a binge. When Kamilah first started, I felt myself bracing for an attack. Everything in me was tensed up tight as a drum.

But the more she talk, the more it made sense. One thing happens and then someone starts feeling sorry for the other one, and the other one feels better because somebody cares. There's people who need and people who need to be needed, and when they get bound up together, it's like a merry-go-round you can't get off. Everybody goin' round and round lookin' for love, but all they get's a glimpse of it goin' by. We need to find a way off this thing or shut it down completely.

I want to make Sister proud of me. I wanna feel like she just wants me around 'cause I make her laugh, not 'cause she scared I'll fall off the wagon and she got to watch so it don't happen.

As tired as I am, I'm feeling something that seems a little bit like hope, and I ain't felt that in a long time.

33 – Patrice

No wonder Kamilah was proud of me this morning. I'd accidentally done what I should have done all along. As much as I complained about Mama enabling Grace, you'd think I'd have seen I was doing the same thing with Miss Ora. She and Mama were the ones who made the decision to cover up a crime, to lie to Gracie, to not report her rape. She was the one who decided to send Marcus off after he killed Skipper. I've been so on edge about having everything dumped in my lap, but I didn't make this mess. Why am I willing to take on the job of cleaning it up? I imagine Mama felt like this a time or two herself.

Then Kamilah asked Miss Ora if *she* thought I was obligated to her for putting me through college and Miss Ora said, "Absolutely not! And I can see where she might think so, because I have certainly behaved like it was my due. But that was never my intent. This is not who I am, or who I would ever choose to be. I need to do better. I will do better."

I started to protest and Kamilah shut me down. "You can do whatever you choose to do in the future, but Miss Ora needs to get herself through this, just like Grace does. Stop taking care of her feelings."

Then she told us a story about a butterfly. As soon as she started, I thought, oh, here we go – a sappy little story that's supposed to enlighten us. I was poised to reject it, but really...it put a whole new perspective on the harmful things we do in the name of helping.

One day a man saw a chrysalis hanging from a bush outside of his living room window. He kept an eye on it for days and was thrilled to finally see a hole appear in its side, and a butterfly struggling to get out. He sat watching for over an hour as the tiny creature pushed against the sides and wriggled back and forth trying to break free. A while later, the butterfly stopped moving, just settled in like she was too tired to keep going. Not knowing much about the life cycles of insects, the man got nervous and scared and decided to help. He got a small pair of scissors, went outside and carefully snipped the remaining shell of the chrysalis off. The butterfly emerged easily then, but it's body was swollen and its legs shrunken in appearance. What he did not understand was that the struggle of freeing itself was designed to force fluids from the body to the wings so they would be ready for flight, and that by removing the natural obstacle, he had crippled the butterfly for life.

I still thought it was a little sappy, but it helped me focus on the ways I've been an enabler, too. I remember feeling terrified when I went off to college. Miss Ora paid for my college, but I had to work to eat, and it was good for me. I learned I had a safety net, but I also had the ability to provide for myself. I had a certain sense of pride that there were some things I didn't have to ask for; I could buy them myself. Don't get me wrong, I wouldn't have made it through law school without Miss Ora's financial help. I was a good student, but the system was the system, and I would not have gotten a full ride to any school, despite my academic achievements.

I think the downside of that experience was that I learned to take on more than most could handle. And when you add that to my sense of blind obligation, it was no wonder I took on Miss Ora's problems as my own.

Kamilah is right. I can be as involved or as detached as I choose. It is my call. And that includes whether or not I'm willing to raise Shawn and Rochelle. Kamilah pointed this out right in front of Grace.

"You may think you don't have options, but you do. You may not like any of them, but there *are* options. You can put them in foster care..."

"Absolutely not." I gripped the arms of my chair and willed myself to stay seated.

Kamilah kept her cool. "I'm not suggesting you do, and I hear you. It would not be a choice I'd want to make either. Still, it is an option."

"I don't want my kids in foster care," Grace said, so softly it was almost like she was talking to herself.

"I hear that, too. The thing is, the program at the Department of Children and Families is *designed* to reunite parents with children. They combine oversight and drug testing and counseling with a clear course of action to regain custody. You guys bypassed that system by stepping in and taking over. Your mother did it, and your sister followed suit. You know these things, Patrice. You work in the system."

"You're right. I know you are, but..." I dreaded even admitting what I was about to say, but it was the truth. "I don't trust the system. I'd rather have taken all the responsibility, just to have control."

Kamilah nodded. "Exactly. But the system requires accountability from the parent, and that's what is missing in this entire equation. Accountability."

"I did try that..." I could feel myself getting defensive again.

"And?" Kamilah asked.

"It's just hard. She needs a roof over her head and food to eat. I never gave her money, though. Mama was the one that did that."

"I'm not placing blame here, Patrice. You've done the best you could in reaction to a very harsh reality – that your sister could die on the streets."

"I don't think it was *that* bad," Grace said.

"Maybe it was and maybe it wasn't," Kamilah acknowledged, "but I can tell you this: at some point you'll have to be honest with yourself if you want to live sober. Regardless, for your own safety and for the wellbeing of this family, we need to have a few common-sense stipulations in place. Look, nobody thinks they're the ones doing the enabling. But if you provide even the most basic needs of an addict – food, clothing, and shelter – you are, in a sense, making it easier for them to use. You are denying them the pain that could very well be their best friend. Pain is a great motivator. If you don't believe me, just look at what it makes good, rational, healthy people do—ruin families, lose jobs, lie, cheat and steal—to get the drugs and alcohol they think helps their pain."

Miss Ora piped up then. She'd been quiet the whole time, just sitting there listening. "I'm confused. If pain is what makes them addicts, how will allowing them to feel pain help? It seems counter-intuitive, doesn't it?"

Kamilah nodded. "It does, but think about it a minute. If you don't allow the natural consequences of addiction to occur in logical sequence, you are disrupting the cycle of recovery. If you provide an addict's basic needs, you make it easier for them to use. In essence, it is less painful to *use* than to get clean. If you allow them to feel the pain that addiction itself causes—loss of jobs, self-esteem, basic comfort, health, food— eventually, that pain becomes the motivator to get well."

"I thought we didn't want to let them hit rock bottom," I said, remembering a previous conversation.

"Bear with me. This is why we lose so many addicts every single day. The families never figure out how to create balance. You can allow consequences without abandoning them completely. And you can help without enabling."

When I glanced over at Miss Ora, she looked as confused as I felt.

"So let me give you a scenario that applies to this family. Is that okay with you, Grace? I'm going to use your situation and give it specifics. These are just suggestions, though. When you all sit down together and develop *your* plan, it will be agreed upon by everyone in the family."

"Go ahead," Grace said without enthusiasm.

"Are you sure?" Kamilah asked.

"Yeah, I wanna hear what you have to say, too. If I don't like it, I'll let you know."

All I could think was, well, at least she's being honest.

"So my recommendation for your family is a contract that sets out reasonable goals and safeguards. Accountability for Grace would include routine and random drug screens. I think you have all agreed you want Grace off the streets and you're willing to provide housing and food, which is great—as long as she stays clean, seeks treatment, and finds meaningful work, whether for pay or as a volunteer. Those things would address a multitude of factors that make Grace want to self-medicate."

"So what do *they* have to do?" Grace was almost sneering.

So much for suspending my anger. I shot up out of my chair so fast, Grace actually flinched. "What do you mean, what do we have to do? We're already—"

"Whoa, whoa, whoa," Kamilah stood with one hand outstretched toward me. "Hang on, Patrice."

It took me a minute to realize my fists were clinched and my arms flexed at my sides. I have no idea what I meant to do. I just knew I was done.

"Patrice, if you need to step out onto the porch and take a few breaths, you can certainly do that. Remember what we talked about."

I caught a glimpse of Miss Ora then. She looked frightened and pale and more fragile than I'd ever seen her. I sat back down and willed myself to be silent and calm.

Kamilah waited a moment and then turned to Grace. "So your question was, what do they have to do. I'm going to turn that back to you, Grace. What do you want them to do? What do you need from them to feel supported and loved."

108

"Well, I mean..." Grace squirmed in her chair and looked back and forth from Miss Ora to Kamilah with an occasional side glance my way. "I know they love me, I just...I don't know...I don't really *need* anything. Obviously, they already supportin' me. I don't know what you want me to say."

"It's not a trick question. I'm asking you to think about what you want from them."

Grace was silent.

"So, let's approach this a different way. Why do you think Patrice reacted so emotionally to your question?"

"She always mad at me. Don't matter what I say, she mad."

Kamilah shot me a pre-emptive warning glance. I bit my tongue.

"Patrice, is she right? Are you always mad at her?"

My first instinct was to deny the accusation. But I thought about it first and responded with as much candor as I could muster. "I've felt angry toward Grace for years now. Am I always mad? No. Not always. But I'm sure it feels like it to her sometimes."

"So now I'll ask you, Grace. What do you want from Patrice?"

My sister's eyes filled with tears and I could tell she was embarrassed by that. "I want her to like me. I want her not to be mad at me all the time. I want her to understand..."

"I want that, too, Gracie," I said, and I meant it.

"And what do you want from Grace?" Kamilah asked me.

"I just want my sister back. I want her happy and healthy. I want her to be able to raise her kids..."

"And let's talk about Shawn and Rochelle for a minute. How do you feel about having the responsibility of raising them?"

That felt like a big fat trap, to be honest.

"I love them," I said, avoiding the question almost entirely.

"That's not what I asked. It's clear you love them. But how do you feel about raising someone else's children?"

"It wouldn't have been my first choice." I felt my heart lurch a bit. I'm not sure I ever thought about what I wanted. The kids were in the picture from the time I got settled into practicing law. They were part of our family and I did what needed to be done to keep DCF out of their lives. They had enough to deal with.

"Did you ever feel like you had options?"

"Sure, I could have let one of the twins raise them, but they were starting families of their own. And I could have let DCF get involved, but up until Mama died, it just wasn't my call."

"And afterwards?" Kamilah pressed on.

"Afterwards, I loved them too much. They'd lost the only two mother figures they'd ever had, and it just seemed cruel to uproot them all over again. But, if I'm being completely honest, I don't actually think I've been that great at parenting. I'm more of a caretaker than a mother, and I think the kids feel that a whole lot more than they let on."

"Do you think your detachment has anything to do with your anger toward Grace for putting you in this position?"

I looked up at Kamilah then. Once again, I wanted to patently deny what felt like an accusation. And I was more than angry that she had asked me in front of everyone. What am I supposed to say?

"That would make me a monster," I said. "And if that's true, then the kids have no business being with me."

"Actually, Patrice, it would make you human. You aren't they're mother. You've done everything any good foster parent would do, and the children are happy and healthy and doing well in school. You're way too hard on yourself." Kamilah smiled at me and turned to Grace.

"So, you asked what Patrice and Miss Ora would have to do as a part of your contract, right? That *is* what you were asking, wasn't it?"

Grace looked uncomfortable. "I guess."

"So how does this sound: Miss Ora will continue to offer a safe haven for you, providing company and support and accountability, sort of like a halfway house. Patrice will continue to care for your children and will work on her feelings of anger and resentment toward you so that your relationship can heal with time. Your part in this is to commit to the things we discussed, with the acknowledgement that, right now, trust has been broken but can be re-earned through your efforts. Does that sound fair?"

I had to think about that question a minute, not because the plan didn't sound fair, but that it sounded far too simple. I didn't think it had a snowball's chance in hell of working.

Grace and Miss Ora just sort of mumbled their agreement, but Grace added, "And what happens if somebody breaks the agreement?"

"Somebody?" Kamilah asked. "I think maybe you mean, what happens if *you* break it."

She shrugged and picked at a piece of lint on her jeans. "Probably so."

"We'll renegotiate if and when that happens. Right now, it's more important that you agree to do your part."

"I'll try," Grace sounded a little half-hearted.

"Either you will or you won't." This was the second time I'd heard Kamilah say this today, and I think I smirked a little. Sounded a whole lot better aimed at someone else than at me.

"The goal here," Kamilah continued, "is self-sufficiency, self-regulation, respect for others, and personal accountability. You do the right thing because it's the right thing, instead of the easy thing because it's easy. I think it's pretty clear that Patrice has reached a breaking point, which would not be good for anyone. So, with that said, I'll set up random drug tests and send the information directly to Grace. It's up to *her* to comply. There is a lab downtown, close enough for Grace to walk."

Now that was something I could agree on. Things need to change, and they need to change soon. The good news is, I think we're all on board. Even Grace.

Kamilah and I filled out paperwork with three different recovery centers, pre-registering Grace so there would be more likelihood of an available bed at a moment's notice. It was as important to plan for success as it was to prepare for the worst.

We've set some ground rules that everyone can live with. It's not my job to get Gracie clean, nor to worry about whether or not she'll choose real help. It is my job to allow her the natural consequences of her actions, to not take away the pain and struggle that may help her achieve *her* goals. It is not my job, but it is my desire, to help her find reasons to want to stay clean. I want my sister back, and I'll do whatever it takes, the right way, to help her get well. So, we have a plan. And we have support. And we have each other. I pray to God that's enough.

Part 3 – June 2001

34 – Patrice

Miss Ora started coordinating her own schedule and stopped relying on me for rides everywhere, but I didn't feel right making her face her legal problems alone. I did feel obligated, but it is not an obligation that I resent. It has become obvious that Miss Ora and I are at odds with each other when it comes to what we expect from the state's attorney. I want to keep her out of jail. She wants to clear Eddie's name.

But there is more to this case than that. Grace told Kamilah there were three other boys involved, not in the rape itself, but they were there when it happened. Seems to me if Miss Ora is going to be held accountable for something she just heard about, those boys ought to bear some responsibility for what they saw and didn't report. I couldn't remember who Skipper hung out with in high school, though. This made me think of Cheryl Kincaid.

We weren't exactly what you would call friends in high school, but we were cheerleaders together, teammates. We became close in college when fate in the form of Ora Lee Beckworth made us roommates. Cheryl was a year behind me, so she moved in when I was a rising sophomore. It was a year or so before I realized we had the same benefactor, which explained a lot.

She was one of those people who just knew everyone. Fit in anywhere. If anyone would remember Skipper's friends, it was Cheryl. It seemed like a good excuse to call her, so I did.

We arranged a time to meet at a local bar and grill for dinner. I had invited her to just stop by Miss Ora's house, but she said there was no way she could do that without her mother tagging along and we both knew that was not a good idea. Miss Dovey was okay, I guess, just hard to take in large doses. I remember she and Miss Ora struggled for years to get along but have since made what amounts to a peace of sorts. They don't seek each other out, but they'll sit and talk on Miss Ora's porch if Miss Dovey catches her out there on her twice-daily walks.

Cheryl is built like her mama, low to the ground and a little wide in the hips, but she carries it well. She is the opposite in temperament, though. Where Miss Dovey is mouthy and quick to judge, Cheryl thinks the best of everyone she meets. She walks through the world loving people just the way they are and assuming they love her back. And they do. Me included.

Cheryl was at the restaurant first and I saw her immediately when I arrived. She came up out of her chair, arms reaching for me before I even got to her. Everyone should have someone who greets them this way. No matter what has happened, you feel like all is right with the world.

"Reese!" Cheryl called out, using the nickname she gave me in college.

We caught up in our usual way, talking over each other. All my training goes out the window, and I become the Patrice I was in school, animated and carefree. At least I was until my brother died. That changed me.

I had thought I would ease into the subject of Skipper's murder gently, but we spent so much time just chatting I was afraid I'd never find a good opening. So when the waitress delivered our second appetizer, I dove right in.

"So," I said, breaking apart a pub pretzel and dipping it into the beer cheese, "what do you remember about Skipper Kornegay getting killed?"

"Oh, gosh," Cheryl tucked her hair behind her ears before tackling the beer cheese with me. "That was a long time ago, Reesie. I've slept since then."

"I know. I've racked my brain, though, and I just cannot remember."

"Well, it wasn't exactly a crowd either of us ran with anyway. Why you studyin' on that right now?"

"Ugh...long story," I said. I wasn't sure I was ready to give her all the details. She's not like her mama, but still, I'm not exactly ready to go public.

"Oh, come on, girl...there's got to be some reason you're askin'. You aren't inclined to waste a syllable, much less a question. What's up?"

I stressed that this was not public knowledge yet and shouldn't be discussed with anyone else. That I was alluding to her mother was a given and she laughed.

"I don't tell that ol' girl nothin'. She's not as bad as she once was, but I still gotta watch what I say."

I told her most of the story, omitting some details and names.

"Well, my Lord, no wonder Grace was so messed up. You know I told Mama one time I didn't know how she'd fallen so far from her little

114

pedestal. I mean, y'all were *all* good people – salt of the earth – but Gracie was such a sweet little thing. It was just hard to imagine her causin' you and your mama so much heartache."

"Makes sense now, but I sure wish I'd known about it a little sooner. It would have changed everything."

"So why you wanna know who Skipper hung out with?"

"Grace says there were three other boys there the day it happened."

Cheryl's eyes got wide. "All of 'em...they were all...oh, God."

"No, no...they were witnesses, that's all. Grace said they came back to find Skipper and saw what he was doing."

"And they didn't stop him?"

I closed my eyes and shook my head. "Apparently they just laughed and told him to hurry."

I should have chosen my words more carefully. Cheryl covered her mouth with her napkin and rushed to the restroom. When she returned, she was pale and clearly stricken.

"I'm so sorry. I don't know what I was thinking, saying it that way."

"Don't you dare be sorry, Patrice. I have my high school yearbooks at Mama's house. I'm gonna get those things and stop by Miss Ora's tomorrow. We are going to figure this out if it's the last thing I do. The very idea..."

This was another thing I've always loved about my friend. She is passionate and determined. If she says we're going to figure it out, we are *going* to figure it out. I tried to change the subject, but she pressed for all the information I knew.

I have to admit I did some soul-searching on the way home. Why haven't I pursued this with the same outrage? This was my baby sister...the victim of one of the most egregious offenses we know. Where is *my* compassion? Kamilah says I need to suspend my anger, but I think it's more than that. I've spent half my life seeing Grace as the perpetrator, and my family as the victim, and the truth is we were *all* victims. Victims of a system that made my mother believe there was no justice to be had for her child. And now, here I am, a part of that system, and what have *I* done to change it?

35 – Grace

Miss Ora and I was plannin' a quiet supper tonight. She hasn't been feelin' all that great, so I told her to head on out to the porch and I'd make us a salad once Patrice'd picked up the kids. I been doin' good, but it's a little strained between me and my babies. Rochelle still lets me help her with homework, and I read to her some, but Shawn, he keep his distance. We made Miss Ora's sewin' room into a little place where they could play video games and watch TV and that keeps 'em pretty happy.

Miss Ora wasn't out there ten minutes 'fore she scooted inside sayin' "Hide me. Dovey Kincaid is headed this way."

I ain't hardly said, "She just go'n knock on the door, Miss Ora. You might as well stayed out there," when sure enough, there came the knock.

But it was Cheryl, not her mama, which was a relief. Unfortunately, Miss Ora done let that relief show plain as a pancake.

"Lord, Cheryl, you look more like your mama every day."

"I'm gonna take that as a compliment, Miss Ora," Cheryl grabbed her by the shoulders and planted a kiss on each cheek. She didn't even turn her loose 'fore she looked her dead in the eye and, with a grin like Alice's cat, says, "Even though I don't think you actually mean it that way."

"Are you forgetting your mama was a debutante?"

"Which means my grandmother thought she was pretty. You might oughta quit while you're ahead." Cheryl turned loose of her then and shot me a *Lord help me* look if I've ever seen one.

I barely had time to think, *this ain't go'n be good*, when Miss Ora laughed so hard she crossed her legs right there in front of God and everybody.

"The older I get, the farther I leave my manners behind. I'm at the point now where I can't hold my water *or* my tongue." Then she headed toward the hallway and spoke without looking back, "You'll have to excuse me on both accounts."

Soon as Cheryl turned her attention to me, I knew Patrice done told her about me. That little twinkle she had laughin' at Miss Ora faded right away.

"Gracie," she said, reachin' both arms out to me. I thought she was gonna hug me, but she took my face in both of her hands and said, "Precious girl...I'm so sorry. I can't even imagine what you've been through. Are you okay?"

Ain't nobody ever asked me that before. Not ever in my life. Anytime Mama'd see me fall, skin my knee, slam my finger in the screen door, whatever, she'd say, "You all right. You fine. Get up now. Go wash your knee. Stick that finger in some water. Put some butter on that burn. You fine, Gracie. Stop that cryin'. It was just a dream. You go'n be fine."

I don't know what came over me when she asked those three little words. Are you okay?

I looked at her for a minute, not sure at all how to answer, and I felt tears rollin' down my cheeks before I even knew I was cryin'.

"I don't know." I said, and that was the honest truth.

***

Miss Ora came back out about the time Patrice got there to pick up the kids, and by then, Cheryl and I was sittin' side by side on the couch talkin' like we was old friends.

Patrice had a bag of groceries and a gallon of milk and she eyed us sideways before she went into the kitchen to put the food away. Miss Ora followed her in there and I could hear 'em whisperin' in there like they didn't want me to hear what they were sayin'. And I couldn't, but I still figured it was about me.

When Patrice came back out, Cheryl said, "You're just in time. Grace and I were just about to look through the yearbooks I brought."

Sister looked confused for a minute. "I thought we were...I didn't mean for Grace to...Grace knows what we're looking for?"

"Well, duh," Cheryl said. "Of course she knows. She's the one who saw 'em in the first place."

"Saw who?" Miss Ora asked from the doorway of the kitchen.

All three of us turned our heads to look at her. Ain't nothin' wrong with her hearin', that's for sure.

117

"The three boys with Skipper. That's who we're looking for, right?" Cheryl leaned over and picked up one of the yearbooks sitting in a stack on the side table.

"Well, yeah," Sister said, "but I was just looking for their names right now."

"Who are you talking about?" Miss Ora had come into the living room by then.

Patrice held up both hands. "Okay, wait. I asked Cheryl last night if she remembered the names of the boys Skipper hung out with in high school. I overheard her telling Kamilah there were two other boys there the day…" She hesitated, so Cheryl finished the sentence for her.

"The day she was raped." I felt her warm hand squeeze my leg just above my knee. It's like she was telling me, *hang on. I got this thing.* "You gotta be able to say this out loud, Reese. Gracie was raped. There is no shame in that. *She's* gotta hear you say it out loud. Y'all can't keep tiptoeing around this thing. That's the biggest problem y'all have right now. Those boys are out there, just goin' on with their lives like nothin' ever happened, but it did. It happened to Grace and it happened to this whole family."

"And you're trying to figure out who they are?" Miss Ora asked.

"Yeah, Patrice and I were going to look through the yearbooks to see if it would jog our memories, but I thought it'd be good if Grace looked, too."

Cheryl just like her mama sometimes. Patrice dropped her shoulders like she was just surrenderin' to the tide that was Cheryl Kincaid. Then Miss Ora dropped her bomb.

"I know their names. I've always known their names."

"You do?" Patrice sat on the couch beside Cheryl and looked up at Miss Ora, who was drying her hands on a kitchen towel.

"Of course, it was…"

"Wait!" Patrice threw a palm up at Miss Ora. "Let's let Grace look first. If she recognizes their faces without knowing their names, she'll be a better witness."

"Good point," Cheryl said.

"Witness for what? They never touched me." I felt myself beginning to shake all over, and I think Cheryl felt it, too. Her hand still resting on my thigh.

"Okay, let's slow down a minute," Patrice said. "I think we're about to run this train off the rails. What are we trying to do here?"

118

We all just kind of looked at each other for a little bit. Nobody seemed to want to answer that question. Finally, it was Miss Ora who spoke.

"All I wanted to do was to tell the truth about Grace. I feel like we owe it to her, and we owe it to Eddie. Really, that's all I ever wanted."

36 ~ Patrice

Grace scanned the 1975 and '76 yearbooks without saying a word. When she got to Skipper Kornegay's class picture, she put her thumb over his face and continued to look at one photo after another. I kept waiting for her to break down, but she didn't.

She also didn't recognize anyone from the tiny rectangular photos covering the pages. We kept thumbing through, though, and finally landed in the sports section. The football team got the biggest spread, of course, being the gods they always were back then. There were plenty of shots of the cheerleaders, too, including me with my glorious Afro and Cheryl with her long blonde ponytail and slightly bowed legs.

"Look how skinny I was." Cheryl looked wistfully at her much younger self. "I would kill to look like that now."

"You and me, both," I said.

"That's how I remember you, Sister. I begged Mama to let me have a 'fro, but y'all kept me in braids all the time. I did *not* think that was fair."

I rolled my eyes. "You think *that* wasn't fair...Mama made me sit there and braid all y'all's hair. One at a time. It took hours."

"Yeah, I know...hours of sittin' there gettin' my hair pulled and twisted. I still hate the smell of Vaseline."

She had a point there. She was the squirmiest of the three girls. The twins would sit still for me, but I always had to let Gracie have several breaks.

"You hated getting your hair done, period." I said. "I'd get three or four rows done, then have to let you run play. I wish I had a picture of you running around with half your hair in cornrows and half of it sticking straight up from your head where I'd combed it all out."

Grace grinned. "I remember that. I'd go to the bathroom and scare myself in the mirror."

We were still laughing at that when Grace turned the page to a half-page photo of Skipper Kornegay and three other boys, arms slung over each other's shoulders. They were all in baseball uniforms, gloves tucked under their arms. Skipper held a bat loosely in one hand, its tip

120

resting on the toe of his cleats. Grace took one look and choked, the sound of her laughter squeezed into a muted wail.

"Oh," Grace leaned back against the couch and squinted at the picture. "Oh, wow."

"Is that them?" I asked.

"That's who I remember him hanging out with," Cheryl said. "They called themselves the Four Musketeers."

Miss Ora was sitting across the room in her recliner. "Allen Madison, Jimbo Hardy and Donnie Allred," she said in a slow monotone.

"Bingo," Cheryl said.

"That's them," Grace said. "I'm pretty sure."

Miss Ora got up and went into the kitchen. We could hear her rummaging around and then it went silent.

"You all right?" Cheryl asked Grace.

Grace shut the yearbook with both hands and slid it onto the coffee table.

"I'm good," she said, then repeated. "I'm good. I don't need to look at 'em again, but I'm good."

"You sure?" I asked.

I heard her say she was okay, but something didn't feel right and the hair stood up on the back of my neck.

"I don't mean to be rude," Grace said, "but I promised to fix Miss Ora and me some supper."

She didn't even look at us then. She went straight to the kitchen. Cheryl and I had just enough time to exchange bewildered glances when Grace yelled from the kitchen.

"Oh my God, Sister! Miss Ora? Sister, call 9-1-1."

37 – Grace

I ain't never been so scared as I was seein' Miss Ora on the floor like that. Her skin was ashy gray and her breathin' was real shallow. I hollered for Patrice and knelt down beside Miss Ora on the floor. I took her wrist and felt for her pulse with my thumb. It was thready, like a' overdose.

"Miss Ora, don't leave me," I whispered. I lifted her head up and pulled her into my lap just as Sister appeared. She had the phone in her hand and was dialing.

"What happened?" she asked me as she put the phone to her ear.

"I don't know. I found her on the floor. She's breathin', but just barely."

I sat there and stroked Miss Ora's hair as I heard Sister talkin' to the dispatcher. It was probably only five minutes before the first responders got there. We're not but a few blocks from the fire department. They had her all hooked up to monitors by the time the ambulance arrived. Actually, Dovey Kincaid beat the ambulance there. Guess she hustled over soon as she saw the firetruck.

Cheryl calmed her mama down while Patrice stayed with me. She made me sit at the kitchen table and focus on breathing calm and slow.

One of the medics asked, "Who's her next of kin?" and Patrice and I both said, "We are."

"You're related to her?"

"Not officially," Patrice said.

"We need next of kin," he said.

"I live here," Grace said. "I'm as close as you're gonna get."

"Do you know what medication she takes?" he asked me.

"Not off the top of my head, but I know where she keeps it. I'll be right back."

I went upstairs to her room and passed the door to Miss Ora's old sewing room. The kids were sitting there, glued to the TV. They hadn't heard a thing. I tiptoed by them and grabbed the plastic box of medicines Miss Ora kept on her bedside table. When I went back by, they both looked up.

"What's going on?" Shawn asked.

I stopped and tried to think of what was a good way to answer him, but I needed to hurry so I just said, "Miss Ora ain't well. Paramedics fixin' to take her to the hospital."

They both jumped up and followed me back down the stairs. I handed the meds off and turned around to make sure the kids were all right. Rochelle tried to go right up to Miss Ora, but Shawn took her by the shoulders and backed her up into a space by the table out of the way. He pulled her close to his chest, wrapped his arms around her and held both of her hands in his. He was saying something into her ear, but I couldn't hear what it was. I went over and stood by my babies.

Rochelle looked up at me just as a tear rolled down her cheek.

"Is Miss Ora gonna be okay, Mama?"

I couldn't help it. I just burst into tears, and only partly 'cause of Miss Ora.

"I hope so, baby," I managed. "I sure hope so."

I put my hand on Shawn's shoulder and he did not pull away.

38 – Patrice

When the ambulance pulled out of the driveway, I picked up the phone and called my Aunt Tressa. It's not like me to call for help, but I knew as sure as I knew my name, I could not handle this on my own. She promised she would work her schedule around so she could be here within a few days. I felt guilty asking her. This was not her cross to bear, but she reassured me as best she could that she *wanted* to come.

My brain raced with details I had to consider, both immediate and long-term. Is Miss Ora dying? Is this the beginning of the end? Will she need care going forward? What about Grace? Will she be okay alone? Where will the kids go after school tomorrow? Does Miss Ora *have* any family to notify? Would she *want* me to notify them? I'd never heard her say a word about a cousin or nephew or niece. Far as I knew, she had no one. I couldn't remember the few details she'd laid out about the house, and I wasn't sure if the trust had even been filed. I didn't even remember the name of her family attorney.

I shook my head of all the noise and called Kamilah next. If I ever doubted her concern for our family, I never will again. She was at Miss Ora's house in less than fifteen minutes. She has such a calming countenance about her, we all breathed a sigh of relief when she arrived.

Bless Dovey's heart, she went straight to the kitchen and started making supper. Cheryl took the kids back upstairs with the promise that we'd let them know as soon as we heard anything. After we ate, Grace and I went to the hospital to check on Miss Ora. Cheryl took the kids to my house. For once in my life, I felt like I had a real support network, like I didn't have to *do* everything for everything to get done.

I expected to hear that Miss Ora'd had a heart attack. In fact, I asked specifically for the cardiac unit and was told she was in the I.C.U. That was another unpleasant experience, explaining to the charge nurse that we were as close to next-of-kin as anyone would get. She wasn't having any of that, though. We were about to give up and go home when one of her care nurses came out and said, "I think she's trying to wake up. She keeps saying something. Sounds like *grace,* but I don't know what she wants."

"That's me," Grace said. "I'm Grace."

So the charge nurse went in and asked Miss Ora herself. We got in to see her with the admonition that we could only stay five minutes. Her speech was garbled, but I could understand most of what she said. She wanted water and Grace helped her take a sip through a straw. I was on her left side and she reached for my hand. She never moved her right hand, though, and the right side of her face seemed frozen. I knew a stroke when I saw one.

I told her Aunt Tressa was coming down, but it would be good if we could clear it with the hospital that we were authorized to visit. She nodded and squeezed my hand.

"Shur-ro-geh," she lifted my hand an inch or so and shook it. "You."

"I'm your medical surrogate?" I asked.

"Yep," she said. Her grin was lopsided and I laughed.

"Thanks for telling me."

"You weh-come." She took a deep breath and closed her eyes. I felt a jolt like an electric current when the exhale was long and full. I was just about to call for the nurse when I noticed her monitor was still beeping softly in rhythm. I looked again and could see her chest rise and fall. She had only gone back to sleep.

Grace kissed her cheek and we tiptoed from the room. I stopped at the desk and told the nurse what Miss Ora had said.

"I don't know if the medical surrogate form is on file here, but I'm certain it would be on file with her regular doctor and cardiologist, so I'll check with them in the morning." I felt grateful for all the times I took her to the doctor's office. At least I knew now where to go.

Grace spent the night with me but insisted on staying at the hospital the next day. She took two books with her and spent the entire day in the ICU waiting room, visiting for five minutes every hour. I stopped by at noon with the medical surrogate papers and was treated like family from then on. I met with the doctors that afternoon and they explained that Mrs. Beckworth was currently able to adequately communicate with them and that they didn't need any particular assistance from me at the time. They assured me they would keep me informed of her care and progress.

The next day, they moved her from the ICU to a regular room and began making plans for a rehab facility when she was sufficiently recovered, which they said could be up to a week.

I didn't change the bus schedule for Rochelle and Shawn. I figured it was just as safe and less confusing if they continued to go to Miss Ora's every day. It's not like they need a babysitter, but they'll be out of school for summer soon. I worry what will happen if Miss Ora never comes home. She's on the mend now, but the doctor warned me it's entirely possible she could suffer another stroke. The underlying problem, a condition called Atrial Fibrillation, wasn't going anywhere. It could happen any time. I need to be prepared for anything.

Aunt Tressa arrived that afternoon. She remembered far more than I did about Miss Ora's legal planning. At this point, we needed to let her personal attorney know and that was it as far as I could tell. Aunt Tressa had arranged to stay a few days, which bought us some time figuring out what to do about Grace. I keep reminding myself what Kamilah said. It isn't my job to keep her off drugs, just to allow for consequences. It's just that the consequences are more than I can bear right now and, besides, Grace has been doing so well. She just passed her first drug screen and I'd really like to keep it that way.

39 – Grace

I know Patrice don't understand why I want to be down here at the hospital all day. There's somethin' in me. Pride I guess. I don't want her to know how hard it is not to use. I been going to AA meetings every single day. There's a couple of churches that have 'em on a regular basis, and I just found out there's one meets right here in the hospital, by the chapel. I can't stand the thought of bein' alone. Miss Ora and I been doin' good together. Settling in as the oddest of couples, but we make each other laugh, and that can't be a bad thing.

Miss Ora the only link I got left to Mama. I feel guilty all the time, if I let myself think about it. All that time I didn't spend with my mother weighs on me – like that time Mama let us go to the beach one day with some neighbors. It was just me and the twins, 'cause Marcus was already gone and Patrice was at college. I was the littlest, so they dug a trench and buried me up to my neck in the sand. It was cool at first – they'd dug deep enough to wrap me in wet sand, and it was a hot summer day. Then they ran down to the water to wash all the sand off their arms and legs and left me with just my head sticking up and the sun beatin' down. I hollered for 'em to get me out, but the sound of the waves and all the other children playin' must've drowned out my cries. The more I struggled the heavier and hotter I felt until I'd have done anything to get outta there. That's how it is with grief. It is so strong, so heavy, that you sweat with the need of something to take you out of it, get it off you so you can breathe again. And dope is like a wave that washes the sand away and leaves you floating in cool, clear water. I gotta find another way to the water or I'm gonna suffocate.

I'll tell you one thing that's the God's honest truth. If they make me stay home one day by myself, I'll use that money in the cabinet. I can't let that happen. I gotta set myself up for success. I gotta change what I can change.

40 – Patrice

Back in college, I learned to duck when Cheryl had one of her big ideas. One time it involved a prank on her sorority sisters by my traditionally black club. I remember thinking *this could go very, very wrong*. But it ended up bringing the leaders of both clubs to friendships that continue to this day.

So when I got a call yesterday, my first thought was that Cheryl had taken matters into her own hands, like her mother always did. She was like a bulldozer – a handy piece of equipment to have in the right hands. Potentially destructive if not.

The call was from Rebecca Yager, a girl we'd grown up with and knew well – Cheryl because Rebecca is white, and I because she is Jewish and suffered some of the same torment I did in elementary school. I was going into the fourth grade when our school board initiated a "trial" desegregation in our county. Marcus and I were both at the top of our class, two years apart. The way the trial worked was that each school would get two or three black children that first year. Brothers and sisters were often sent together, which is what happened to us. I entered the fourth grade and Marcus the sixth at Skiles Elementary School, an otherwise all-white school, in the fall of 1968.

No one could have prepared us for what happened that year, but Mama did try. Daddy was still alive then and working at the citrus plant on the night shift. They bused us across town to the new school. We were the last to get on and the first to get off that bus every day, which was a miracle when I think of it now. I remember the first day – Mama walking us up the long front walk to meet the principal. She was a compact, forbidding looking woman with a beehive hairdo that made her seem taller than she was. She sat us down and told us she was glad we were there and that she expected us to love the school. I remember Marcus made a funny noise when she said that, and Mama elbowed him. I was kind of excited to do something new. Marcus was furious. He didn't want to be there at all. He wanted to be back at his own school with his own friends. In my profound naivety, I looked at it like an adventure and it was, though not always in a good way. Of course, when I look back on it now, I am in awe of the courage it took my mother to leave us at a school where we would be tolerated at best, and Lord only knew at worst.

Miss DeAngelo talked to Mama for a bit and asked if she had any questions or concerns. I'll never forget the one question Mama asked her, "How you go'n keep my children safe?" That's when it hit me, I guess.

"Mama?" I said, looking up in alarm.

She put her hand on my arm. Her white glove glowed against the dark of my skin.

"Shhhh, child," she whispered.

Miss DeAngelo looked Mama straight in the eye and said, "Mrs. Lowery, I know you don't know me, but I hope you'll trust me when I say this. I'm determined to make this work. I believe this is the right thing – for our schools and for our country – and I will do everything in my power, not just to keep them safe, but to make this a good experience for them. You have my word."

Then she turned to us and told us she would be checking on us all the time, but if we had any problems at all, we should tell our teachers. If they didn't handle it, she said, we should come straight to her office as soon as we could and she would take care of everything. This included, she was careful to add, any name-calling or threats or physical violence.

"What's violence mean?" I asked.

"If anyone hurts you," she said.

Later that day, I looked up the word in my new teacher's fat red dictionary. It sat right on the corner of her wide wooden desk, like a beacon to my language-loving soul. She asked me why I was looking it up and I remember telling her I just didn't like it when I didn't know how to spell a word or know what it meant. She smiled at me then, and her face transformed.

"Patrice Lowery," she said, "I think you and I are going to be good friends."

And that was the end of my fear, if not my struggles. I did have to go see Miss DeAngelo a few times, mostly for minor slights, but I also learned to take up for myself. Rebecca Yager was the one to thank for that.

The thing was, the first time a kid called me a name, I wasn't even sure he knew it was wrong. He used the word like it was just another noun. There's the water fountain. There's the pencil sharpener. There's the nigger.

Rebecca leapt from her chair and slapped the boy right across the face.

"What'd ya do that for?"

"I'll do worse if you ever call her that again," she said.

"I don't think he meant anything by it," I offered lamely. Is it any wonder I became a defense attorney?

She wheeled on me like she was going to slap me, too, and I flinched.

"Oh, don't be stupid, I'm not going to hit you." She leaned in close then, placing both palms flat on my desk. "You can't give these jerks an inch, kid. You ride bus 38, right?"

I nodded.

"I sit halfway back...fourth seat on the left. I'll save you a spot today."

I took that as an order of sorts and I sat with her every single day that year, though I soon realized she didn't actually have to "save" me a seat. No one ever sat with her. I never figured out if it was because she was Jewish or because everyone was terrified of her. She'd just as soon smack someone as look at them, and she never got in trouble for it, either. Far as I could tell, no one ever told on her. Not the boy slapped on my behalf, or the girl whose foot she stomped for trying to warn her that someone was trying to "Jew her down." Our class got schooled in political correctness before it was a popular term. Corporal punishment was part of her lesson plan.

We ended up in a different class the next year, and completely different schedules once we hit high school. I still knew her, but we didn't run in the same crowds. The last thing Rebecca Yager would be was a cheerleader like me. She was on the debate team and served two years as president of the National Honor Society. She was the only girl I knew who wore corduroy blazers and loafers with bright copper coins tucked into the penny slots.

When she called, she said she'd learned about some irregularities in the case of the Pecan Man and was looking for more information for a story she was writing. I did my best to find out where she'd gotten the lead in the first place, but she never gave it away. Not even a pronoun slip. I agreed to meet with her at Miss Ora's house that evening after I picked up Grace from the hospital. It's Gracie's story. It's best if she's the one who tells it.

41 – Grace

When I first heard about a reporter wantin' to write my story, I was sure it was Cheryl's doin' and I didn't want any part of it. She swore to me, though – and I think I believe her – that she was not the one who called this Rebecca girl. I ain't all that excited about the whole world knowin' my business, but on the other hand, I'm tired of hidin'. Tired of everything *but* the truth bein' told around me and about me.

I decided right off the bat I was gonna own up to everything I did. It's like I have a chance to start over. Not just a do-over though. It's a rewrite. Start from the beginning and tell the truth, even the things I did wrong.

The other day at an AA meeting somebody said, "If I will not take responsibility, I cannot take control." I thought to myself, that's the truest thing I ever heard. All this time I been blaming everybody else, when wasn't nobody gonna step in and fix my life for me, even if they *did* screw it up. I'm tired of not having control over my life, my body, my story. It's time to change the thinking that keeps me from changing.

They moved Miss Ora from intensive care to a regular room today, so I can stay in there with her. I brought one of her favorite books and read to her for a little bit. She loves Ferrol Sams. We're on *The Whisper of the River* right now, but that's the second one. I swear sometimes it makes me laugh right out loud.

She still can't talk right, but I'm gettin' to where I can understand her okay. She don't need much, but she's askin' can she get her hair done. The nurse brought me some dry shampoo in a spray can and I did my best to make it look right, but I don't know what to do with hair that fine. It flattens out in the back and don't hold any curl at all at the top. Miss Ora always gone to the beauty parlor once a week where they wash it and set it and it stays lookin' the same 'til she goes again next week. I told her I'd call her hairdresser and see can she come by after work one day.

Then I told her about the reporter and she looked at me all worried-like.

"Patrice and Cheryl know her from high school. They said she'd do a good job," I tried to console her.

"Izzat what you wan'?" She has to work hard to make her mouth do right. I feel bad makin' her talk, but the nurse said it was good for her to try.

I shrugged my shoulders. "I'm all right with it. Almost feels like it's settin' me free in a way. I know – that just sounds weird. I can't really explain it."

She reached for my hand. "I geh it. I prou' of you, Gracie."

I figured now was as good a time as any, so I took a deep breath and let it out.

"You wouldn't be proud of me if you knew what I did, Miss Ora."

She looked at me for a minute. I thought she might cry, but she didn't.

"You wan' teh' me?" She squeezed my hand. "Ih okay, you teh' me."

I felt so ashamed, I knew I had to just spit it out or I'd never tell.

"You know that money you had in the pantry?"

Her eyes got dark and she shook her head side to side.

"In the baking powder jar. It's a big ol' wad of Ben Franklins."

She looked confused, but then I could see a wave of memory wash across her face.

"I forgah' aw abou'... Wwwwal...my husban'...he call it ma' money."

"Mad money?"

"Yeah. He say he puh' sumpin' in it ev' time he make me mad. Say he go'n take me somwheh' to spen' it someday."

"That was a lot of money. You musta stayed mad at him."

"Noooo..." she laughed. "Jus' a joke. I teh' you abou' him someday."

"Where was he gonna take you?"

"He say Ha-why-ee, buh' I nev' wan' fly, so we nev' go." She laughed a little, then her face got serious again. "How you know abou' money?"

"I found it, Miss Ora. I spent some of it. On drugs. And I'm telling you now because I want to get better. I want to do better, Miss Ora. I'll pay you back, I promise."

She shook her head back and forth. "I not worry abou' money, Grace. I worry abou' you."

"I worry about me, too, Miss Ora."

I scooted my chair closer to her bed and laid my head on the mattress by her shoulder. She held my hand in her good hand, patting it every now and then until we both fell asleep. We were still asleep when Sister stopped by to take me home.

42 – Patrice

There are some people in this world you love to hate, and some you hate to love. Rebecca is one of the latter for me. I remember her as brash and opinionated, and always raging against perceived injustices. As a child, I loathed the sound of her voice, tinny and sharp-edged, but I secretly applauded her bravado.

After she told me she was researching a story about Eddie, I did some research and found some articles she had written. Her work is well-crafted, her stories compelling.

On the ride home from the hospital, I warned Grace about my old friend.

"I think she'll do a good job," I said. "But I'm not sure at all that you'll actually like her. She's a little hard to take sometimes."

"I don't care if I like her or not, long as she gets the story right."

"I trust her, if that helps."

Grace didn't say anything for a few minutes. She just stared out the car window and picked absently at the cuticle on her thumb. When we pulled into the driveway, she got out of the car and walked straight to the back door. By the time I made it through the back porch and into the kitchen, she had a small tin canister in her hand.

"Take this," she said. "I told Miss Ora how much I spent and how much I owe her, and now I'm telling you. I can't stay clean if I know it's there."

I pulled the plastic lid off and looked inside at the rolled-up bills.

"How long have you had this?"

"Long enough," she said.

"Have you broken the contract?" I could feel the heat rising in the back of my neck. All I could think was, *not now. Dear God, not now.*

"No!" Her answer was swift, but I'd heard it before. "That's why I'm giving it to you. You can test me. We can go right now."

I heard Kamilah's voice in my ear. *Lead with love. Give her a reason to want to get well.*

"We can go in the morning," I heard myself say. "That way we'll both know we did the right thing. This is good, Grace. You can tell me later how much you owe Miss Ora."

I swear I saw my baby sister rise up two inches taller.

"I been thinkin' a lot about how much I owe everybody. If I try too hard to work it out in numbers, it gets overwhelming. I can't give you back the years you've spent raisin' my kids. I can only focus on the examples y'all set for me. I need to stay busy, Sister. That money been callin' to me every day, and I been proud every day I didn't use it. But I didn't wanna give it up. Kinda like a safety net, you know? But that ain't right thinkin'. So I want you to put that money away now. I'm gonna step up and take care of things like I should. The kids is out of school next week for summer break. I want 'em here every day. And when Miss Ora get outta the hospital, I can take care of her here. I can do it, Sister. I need to do this."

I reached out and hugged Grace tight. I was so afraid I'd say the wrong thing, I said nothing at all. I'm afraid she'll take on more than she can handle, but I don't want to discourage her. If she believes she can do it, maybe she will.

***

Grace went upstairs to help Shawn and Rochelle with their homework while I waited for Rebecca to arrive, which she did about a half an hour later. She is the same in many ways, but different. She is calm, assured, pleasant, but still distant and wound pretty tight.

"So how'd you say you found out about this story?" I tried to sound nonchalant, but I'm certain I failed.

She narrowed her eyes and laughed – more like snorted. "I didn't say," she said, taking out a leather-bound notebook and pen. "And I'm not going to say. If that's a deal-breaker, tell me now. I'll do it without you."

Lordy, same old Rebecca, no doubt.

We chatted briefly about high school and college and the fact that neither of us had married, which made me curious.

"I saw your byline. You go by Yager-Mills now?"

"I have a partner," she said, flipping open her notepad. "We both hyphenated."

"Ah, what's her name? Anyone I know?"

Rebecca stopped and studied me over the top of the pad for a few seconds. "Maybe. You remember Debbie Mills?"

135

"Hah!" I slapped my thigh. "I *knew* that's who you were going to say. I do remember her! Do you still stomp on her foot when she makes you mad?"

Rebecca laughed so hard, she started coughing.

"Damn cigarettes," she said, still hacking. "I can't believe you remember that."

"Girl, I remember a lot. I was in awe of you."

"The feeling's mutual," she said with the first smile I'd seen on her face today. What an amazing thing a smile can do. I'd never thought of Rebecca as pretty before.

She took out a digital recorder and put it on the table in front of me. "Mind if I record?"

"Not at all. Let me go get Grace, though," I said, standing. "I'd really like for her to tell you her story."

"I'd rather talk with you separately, if that's all right."

I sat back down. "Okay, sure. I don't know a lot, only what I've been told, really."

"That's fine," she said. "This can be a little tedious, but it works better for me to hear from one person at a time."

Rebecca leaned forward and pressed a button on the recorder.

"Rebecca Yager-Mills, Interview with Patrice Lowery, Attorney-at-law, May 26, 2001. Miss Lowery, I am taping this interview for future use in an article or articles to be written by me. If you agree to the interview, please state your name and occupation and your consent to record our conversation."

I answered her questions as best I could, and I soon realized she already knew some of the answers. It bothered me not to know who she'd spoken to first. I'd done depositions before, but this was different. I felt awkward. I train my clients to answer only the question asked, but this was the opposite of what Rebecca hoped from me. Eventually I relaxed and it felt more like conversation than interrogation.

She asked me very little about the things I'd heard secondhand. She focused more on what my childhood was like, who my mother was, and what kind of brother Marcus was. I was honest with her. My childhood was pretty idyllic, from my perspective anyway, until my father died when I was ten. His mother, my grandmother, was living with us at the time and she took it harder than all of us. She was the only grandparent I ever knew, and she only lasted about four years after Daddy died. That was when I had to grow up and start taking care of things. From

136

that time on, I watched Gracie every day after school while Mama worked. She'd get home about four or five every day and fix supper, but for two years, Marcus and I coordinated our schedules to make sure someone was home to take care of Grace. We never fought about it, either. It was just the way things were. Every now and then, we'd have to ask one of the neighbors to watch her for an hour or so after she got off the bus, but I'm pretty sure there was a time or two when she went home to an empty house for a little while. Our world was safe, normal, happy. Even when I was home, Grace spent half her time off in the neighborhood, playing with her friends. I think I told her these things to justify why I let her walk to Miss Ora's by herself. Rebecca took notes and asked occasional leading questions.

"What do you remember about the day your brother died?"

"Very little," I said. "We were all devastated, especially Gracie. She would wake up calling for him every night. The twins took it hard, of course, but they had each other. I felt like I was the one really left stranded."

"So you were close?"

"Very. I idolized him. But I was also the one who had to be strong. Mama grieved, of course, but she was always stoic. I remember crying about something one time and she told me I'd cried enough and I needed to stop. It was one of the few times I talked back to my mother. I told her she hadn't cried once since the funeral and she must not even miss Marcus. 'Don't you worry about whether or not I cry,' she said. 'I buried my son. You come back and tell me what I oughta do when you bury one of *your* children.' That's how Mama was. She knew exactly what to say to make you regret opening your mouth. Of course, I know now that Mama was heartbroken. I knew she changed some after Daddy died, but after Marcus...well, she was a different person altogether. It was like she built a fortress around her that no one was going to get through. She loved us, though. No doubt about that."

I heard Grace coming down the stairs then and realized Rebecca and I had been talking a full hour. I stood then and greeted my sister.

"I'm going to go in and make us some supper while you talk to Rebecca. The kids are probably starving."

"They claim they are, but I know better." She took a deep breath and let it out at once. "Okay, let's get this show on the road."

43 – Grace

That Rebecca girl is somethin' else. I don't think I'd wanna be alone in an alley with her, that's for sure. It's a little hard to read her and we were quiet at first. She was fiddlin' with her recorder like it wasn't working right or something.

"I'm just a little curious about all this," I said. "What's your plan?"

"My plan?" She seemed irritated by the question.

"Yeah, like, why are you doing this?"

"Same reason I always have – to tell the story. I have no ulterior motive, Miss Lowery, if that's what you mean. I was asked to write the story, and that's what I'm going to do."

"Who asked you?" I demanded.

"Technically, my boss," she said. "I got the lead directly, but I had to clear it with him first."

"Directly from whom?" I asked again.

"Miss Lowery, I'll tell you like I told your sister. I do not divulge any sources at all. Not ever. I just don't."

I stared at her a minute. Some people just full of themselves.

"Fine, but I don't know who you're talkin' to when you say Miss Lowery. I'm just Grace."

She said, "Fair enough," and started right in. She asked for my name and occupation, and that bugged me just enough to get smart with her. "Grace Lowery, Recovering Drug Addict. You can record whatever you want. Don't matter to me."

I figured out pretty quick she don't react to nothin' I say, so I got ahold of myself and started talkin' straight. She ain't bad, really. She just serious as all get-out.

So I ended up tellin' my story all over again, which ain't easy, especially when you're talkin' to a stranger.

"So tell me about the boys on bicycles," she said. "Had you ever seen them before that day?"

"I don't remember. If I did, I didn't pay 'em no mind."

"Did you see them after the rape?"

I had to think about that a minute.

"Seems like I did, but it's all confusing. I didn't think I'd be able to pick them out of the yearbook, but I recognized 'em right off. I remember a time or two I kinda freaked out. Once when I saw that white-haired boy and another time when I saw some boys on bicycles downtown. I don't know if they were the same ones or not. You gotta understand, my mama told me the rape never happened, that I just dreamed it. I grew up tryin' to make myself believe her."

"Why do you think she told you that?" Rebecca stopped writing in her notebook and looked hard at me.

"Miss Ora say it's 'cause Mama didn't think the police'd believe me. Knowin' what I know now, I'd say she prob'ly right. But I also think *Mama* the one didn't wanna deal with it. She was scared for me, but she was scared for the whole family, includin' herself. And there was Marcus off at boot camp and us girls always home alone. No tellin' what they'da done to us back then. Just no tellin'."

"So you went twenty-five more years thinking you'd had a nightmare instead? You didn't question that at all?"

I 'bout came up outta my chair. "Girl, come on," I said. "Of course I questioned it. I questioned it every day. Sometimes out loud, sometimes just in my head. It never made sense to me, but eventually Mama stopped answering my questions. 'Enough about that dream,' she said. 'How many times I tol' you? Stop askin' me all the time.' And I finally stopped asking. But I never stopped questionin'. I didn't get the real answer 'til Mr. Pecan died."

"How'd you feel after that?"

"About like you'd imagine, if you actually *could* imagine. I loved my mother, and I love Miss Ora, but I felt betrayed in the worst way. I guess I got a little of my mama in me, 'cause at some point you just have to let it go. *Stop studyin' on it*, as Mama used to say."

"Can we talk a little about your substance abuse?" She just throws stuff in the air to see where it lands, I think.

"What do you wanna know?"

"When did it start? How old were you? Why do you think you were drawn to drugs? That kind of thing."

I rubbed the back of my neck and stretched.

"Somebody at my AA meeting the other day called it *unresolved business*. I think that's exactly it. I had some issues I never addressed. I didn't even know how to address them, you know? It's like a ghost standing in your living room. You can see it there, and it's jumpin' out at ya' goin' *boo!* But nobody else sees it, and it ain't like you can pick it up and move it. So, you just live with it as long as you can. Then one day you figure out that you can't see it either when you're high. So you get high and you feel better for a little bit. But then you open your eyes and there sits the ghost, laughin' his ass off."

She actually smiled then. "I like your analogies. Do you write?"

I had to study her a minute to see if she was makin' fun of me, but she seemed serious.

"I journal some, and I used to write really bad poetry, but no, not really."

That wasn't actually true, but I didn't feel like sharing anything with her, so I lied.

"So, I think we can stop here." Rebecca leaned up and turned off the recorder, then stood and stretched.

Patrice came in then, wiping her hands on a towel. "Can you stay for supper? I've got plenty."

"No, but thank you. Deb's cooking tonight. I'd best get home."

"So how'd we do?" Patrice asked her. "Do you need to talk to Miss Ora? It will be a while, but I can set it up when she's able."

"I think I'm good for right now. Maybe later. I have a little research to do. I've pulled some of the police reports, one on your brother's accident and a couple on the Kornegay murder. It will take me a while on some of that investigation."

"I've never seen the report on Marcus's wreck. Do you mind sharing it with me later?" Patrice put the towel down and followed Rebecca to the door.

I went upstairs to get Shawn and Rochelle while they said their goodbyes. They were still talking when we came back down. Rebecca came at me with her hand stuck out, so I shook it.

"Thanks for being so forthright with me today. I gotta say, you're kind of a breath of fresh air," she said.

"I hope that's a good thing," I said.

Shawn and I started getting food to the table while Patrice walked her out to her car.

"Who's that?" Rochelle asked me the second the front door closed.

"She writes for the newspaper," I said. "You wash your hands?"

She froze for a second, then went to the kitchen sink to wash up.

Shawn got the plates out of the cabinet but stopped before he passed me on the way to the dining room. "They writing a story about you?"

"Kinda," I said. "Mostly about Mr. Pecan, I think. I wish you'da known him, Shawn."

"What was he to me?" Shawn asked.

"He was your great-granddaddy." And he was great, I thought to myself. A great man.

44 – Patrice

Grace passed a drug screen the next day. We had decided to send her for random tests at the lab, which they would call for and conduct, and she's had one so far, which she also passed. This time we used the over-the-counter brand we'd bought for emergencies. My instinct was to say, "It's okay, I believe you," but I followed the plan instead, and was relieved to have evidence rather than doubt or suspicion.

We called a family meeting for the next evening, to include our twin sisters Danita and Re'Netta, Grace, Aunt Tressa and Kamilah. Miss Ora was still in the hospital but scheduled to go to a skilled nursing facility soon where they offered on-site physical therapy. The stroke was fairly mild, I was assured, but she needed help recovering some fine motor skills. Already her speech was improving and her face was almost completely unfrozen.

Danita brought her two children Alex and Mica, who are close in age to Shawn and Rochelle. Because of the situation with Grace, the cousins grew up spending a lot of time together but haven't gotten to see each other as much since Mama died. The first thing they did was head upstairs to "their room" as they now call it.

As soon as the twins arrived, I was filled with nostalgia and longing for...well...I was going to say the good old days, but that seems a bit optimistic. On the other hand, we did have good times. There was a lot of laughter in our family, at our home and here at Miss Ora's.

"Feels weird here without Miss Ora," Re'Netta said. She'd come into the kitchen with me to help me get a tray of drinks for everyone.

"It does," I agreed. "I asked Miss Ora if she wanted me to take Grace to my house and she said, 'absolutely not.' I think she was worried about her house being empty, if you want to know the truth."

"When is she coming home?" Re'Netta cracked an ice tray and started to fill the glasses lined up on the counter.

"Soon, I hope. That's really what we're meeting about tonight. Just where to go from here and what to do about Grace and the kids. I have a full schedule this summer. I'm a little worried about how we'll manage everything."

We finished our work and headed for the dining room where everyone was seated and chatting. Aunt Tressa had landed at the head of the table, which felt fitting somehow. I hadn't known her long, but her presence was a comfort to me. Grace sat to Aunt Tressa's left and Kamilah to her right. Danita was next to Grace, her arm already forming a protective circle around Grace's shoulders. Re'Netta placed the tray of iced tea and water glasses in the center of the table and took a seat at the other end.

Before we could start the meeting, the doorbell rang, and I got up to answer it. Dovey Kincaid didn't wait for me to invite her in, she just stepped across the threshold the second I swung the door back.

"What's happened? I saw all the cars. Is it Mrs. Beckworth? Is she okay?"

"Hey, Miss Dovey," I said by way of greeting. "She's fine. We're just having a family meeting to discuss what's going to happen when she comes home, that's all."

Lord help me, that woman flung herself into the nearest wing chair, picked up a magazine from the coffee table and started fanning herself.

"Thank God," she said. "I thought maybe she died. I just couldn't stand it. I had to know."

I closed the door and stood there a moment trying not to laugh at her dramatics.

"Uh, is there anything else, Miss Dovey? We were just about to start our meeting."

She sat up straight, then reached down and tugged at the back of one of her polka-dot Keds. She was still tugging when she looked up at me like she just had a bright idea.

"Hey, how 'bout if I sit in for a bit? I know y'all are gonna need more help when she comes home."

I know my mouth had to have been hanging halfway open, because I just could not make it form words from the thoughts racing through my head. This woman is crazy. How can she...? What do I...? What do you say...?

The doorbell rang again. I opened it a crack to see Cheryl standing a foot from the door. I stuck my head out.

"Is she here?" Cheryl whispered.

"Yep," I said, my eyes raised in mock distress.

"Oh, God," she clapped her hands over her cheeks. "Was she invited?"

"Nope," I whispered back.

Cheryl pushed the door open and brushed past me.

"Mama? Mama, what in the world are you doing here?" she demanded.

"I'm just tryin' to help, Cheryl Lynn. Don't be rude."

"You're the one being rude. You just come home right now. We are not going to interrupt these people in the middle of…" She looked at me in horror. "What are y'all doin'? Has something happened?"

I couldn't help it. I laughed out loud.

"What's so funny?" Cheryl wailed like she was afraid to hear the answer.

"Miss Ora is fine. We're just meeting with everyone to figure out the best way to move forward. It was easier to hold the meeting here. That's all. We've got to plan for Miss Ora to come home, and she's going to need help."

"Well, that's why I'm here," Miss Dovey said. "I wanna help y'all."

I nodded. "I know you do, and that is very kind of you. I will let you know as soon as I know exactly how you *can* help. Will that work?"

"Well, I was just…" Dovey said.

"That will work fine," Cheryl interrupted. "Come on, Mama. It's time to go home."

Cheryl pushed her mother toward the porch and mouthed *I'm sorry* over her shoulder as she closed the front door behind them.

I was still chuckling when I got back to the table.

"What was *that* all about," Re'Netta asked.

"Oh, Miss Dovey thought maybe Miss Ora had died." I rolled my eyes upwards. "That woman."

"She means well," Grace said, and we all burst into laughter. Miss Ora instructed us long ago this was just about the worst thing you could ever say about someone.

"Cheryl came and got her. I honestly believe she wants to help, which is wonderful. But family meetings are for family." I pulled out my chair and sat back down beside Kamilah. "What'd I miss?"

"Grace was just telling us she passed another test yesterday," Kamilah said. "Super good news there."

I wasn't sure whether to bring up the money or not. I didn't want to embarrass her, but it was an important part of the story.

"I told 'em about the money, too, Sister."

The way she said it, I figured she read my mind. She sounded a shade resentful.

"You both did exactly the right thing," Kamilah said. "You followed the plan. Grace is stepping up, and you are stepping back. This is how it works. Proud of both of you."

Grace and I looked at each other then and we both smiled. The thought crossed my mind that this was the first positive thing we had shared in a long, long time, and the relief was palpable.

It didn't last long, but I still cling to the experience as something I want to recreate.

Aunt Tressa shuffled a stack of papers and cleared her throat.

"Patrice asked me here to help with any legal matters that might come up now or in the future. I was able to meet with her family attorney yesterday at the hospital. He has been overseeing the details of her living trust and is currently a joint trustee with Mrs. Beckworth. She has decided to go ahead and make Patrice a co-trustee with Mr. McClellan instead of herself. That's the biggest legal change right now. Well, that and the fact that Patrice has also been given a Durable Power-of-Attorney to handle her business affairs while she is incapacitated. For now, we wanted to figure out how to handle the running of Mrs. Beckworth's household and her healthcare when she is allowed to come home. I don't want to tiptoe around this, so I'm going to be blunt. The issue includes Grace's recovery and the care of her children, especially over the summer. Patrice has, of course, been their guardian and caregiver, and will continue to be. But with everyone working full-time, it seems prudent to parse out a few things amongst all of you so that no one is bearing too great a burden." Aunt Tressa paused for a minute and the table was silent. "Now's your time to chime in. Any suggestions?"

Danita piped up then. "I'm happy to help. I'm only working part-time this summer down at the Y, and Alex is lifeguarding there. We figured Mica can hang out and swim when we're working, but she also has church camp for two weeks. We could see if Shawn and Rochelle want to go, too. It's up in the mountains. Mica loves it."

"I'm definitely working full-time, but it gets slow in the summer at the salon. I could take Rochelle a couple of days a week if she didn't mind hanging out at the shop." Re'Netta laughed then as if she just thought of something funny. "I was going to say Shawn, too, but ain't no way he'd be happy listenin' to the hens chatter all day."

145

"I bet I can get him a job as a lifeguard. We still have some openings," Danita said.

"I could also come by after work a couple of days a week and help Miss Ora a little," Re'Netta offered. "I could do her hair for her, help her take a bath or pay some bills, whatever she needs. How much do you think she'll be able to get around? I feel bad I haven't been by the hospital, but with all the prom and graduation stuff, it's just been real busy at the salon. And I can make at least a meal or two a week. That'd be nice, I think. I could spend a little time with Miss Ora and Grace and the kids. I'd like that."

I noticed Grace starting to fidget when Re'Netta started talking. Aunt Tressa apparently noticed, too.

"What is it, Grace? Do you want to say something?"

"Am I *allowed*?" Her voice was thick with sarcasm. It seemed to drag all the goodwill out of the room.

"Grace!" I snapped. "What is wrong with you?"

"I *live* in this house. I live here 'cause Miss Ora asked me to and y'all actin' like I ain't even in the room."

Kamilah sat up a little straighter but didn't speak right at first.

I glared at her. "Did we ignore you? Did we *tell* you not to speak? If you have something to say, say it. It's a *family* meeting. Nobody stuffed a sock in your mouth."

Kamilah put a hand on my leg, but still didn't speak. Aunt Tressa looked uncomfortable, and Danita patted Grace on the shoulder in a soft random rhythm. I took a deep breath.

"I'm sorry," I said. "I *don't* think anyone was ignoring you, though. If you have suggestions, we'd like to hear them."

Grace did not respond, just sat staring at her hands in her lap.

Kamilah rose from the table then. "Grace, can we chat just a minute? Maybe out on the porch?"

She waited for Grace to rise, then followed her silently out of the room.

"What was that all about?" Re'Netta asked.

I sighed. "I want to say I don't know, but I think I do. And I'm not even sure she's completely wrong. She has always been the baby of the family. I think she just wants to be treated like an adult."

I'm not sure where that even came from, but the four of us sat with it for a few minutes before we started talking about Miss Ora again.

45 – Grace

Kamilah followed me out to the porch and we sat there for a minute just rocking.

"You want to tell me what's going on?" she asked finally.

"Why doesn't anybody think I can handle taking care of my own kids? Why can't they just stay here with me and Miss Ora this summer?"

She hesitated like she was thinking, then let out a big sigh. "Grace, you are doing so well, and I am proud as I can be of your progress…"

"But what?" I asked.

"But I don't think you're there yet. I've seen this so many times and I'm afraid that much responsibility could undo all the work you've done. Nobody is saying you can't pitch in with Miss Ora. There's a lot you can do. What they're trying to do is help you so nobody is overwhelmed."

"I won't be overwhelmed. I can do this."

"I believe you can. But I don't think it's the best thing for you *or* your children. We need more history of success first. That's the way this works. You create a new history with time and consistent behavior. So, the fact that you are pushing for something you haven't earned is actually concerning to me. I'm asking you to trust me. I'm asking you to consider that those women in there – your family – are there to help you. Let them do this. You concentrate on yourself right now."

I wish I could make her understand how much I want to be well this time, but I can't. I have to show her. This is what she's telling me. And yet, my blood just boils from aggravation. Everybody thinks they know better than me, but they ain't in my head.

"Okay," I said. "I get it. But could you talk to them about lettin' me take care of Miss Ora? I need to feel good about myself. I need to feel like I can make a difference to somebody. I can't explain it. I just need it."

"You don't need anyone's approval to do that, Grace. When Miss Ora gets here, you can do whatever you like. If they hire someone to do it and it's already done, you'll have shown them you are reliable and determined. Don't ask for permission. Just do it."

We talked for a little more and then went back inside to finish our meeting.

I started to get mad all over again when I realized they didn't wait on us. They'd already decided a schedule and everything. But then Patrice said it was just *ideas* for a schedule and what did I think about it. I studied it a minute 'fore I said anything. Looked like they did have some time where I was there with Miss Ora and the kids. Problem was, it was mostly in the mornings.

"Well, I guess one thing that worries me is my AA meetings. I been goin' every day around lunchtime. I'm wondering how much time she can be left alone, 'cause I don't want to miss any meetings. I can go at night if I need to, but it's a little scary walkin' after dark."

Re'Netta looked at me funny for a second. "Why are you going to AA? Shouldn't it be the one for narcotics?"

Kamilah scrunched her face up. I think she thought that was gonna upset me, but it didn't.

"I prefer the AA meetings. It's hard bein' around other addicts. There's always somebody there been ordered by the court and they'd just as soon sell you somethin' as get clean."

"Ohhhh," she said. "I never even thought of that."

Kamilah winked at me then. "I like the way you're thinking, Grace."

I couldn't even keep the smile off my face. I like feeling good about myself for a change.

Aunt Tressa got us back on track. "So some of this is going to depend on how Mrs. Beckworth is feeling when she gets home, but there shouldn't be a problem working out your meetings, Grace. Certainly, they are a priority."

"Don't forget that Miss Dovey offered to help some. Maybe she could come over and sit while you go," Patrice said.

I 'bout busted out laughing. "That'll make Miss Ora wanna get well, won't it?"

We all got tickled then.

"Any port in a storm." Aunt Tressa had her mouth all tight like it was all she could do not to laugh. She all dignified most of the time. I'd give a lot to see her cut loose jus' once."

We got as much settled as we could not knowing when Miss Ora would be coming home, then we jus' sat around and talked like old times 'til the kids come down hungry and squabblin' over who had the most points on some game I ain't never heard of. Patrice ordered pizzas and the kids went out back with me to help me deadhead the tea roses and water the garden while it was still light and halfway cool outside. I planted tomatoes out there last month and they comin' in good now.

I've never been good at bein' patient. I think that's part of bein' an addict. You want what you want when you want it. But I'm not in control of when I get my children, so I'm gonna do what Kamilah say and just try to prove I can do it.

46 – Patrice

We moved Miss Ora to a facility close to town so Grace can walk down to visit when she wants to. It would be easier for everyone if Grace had a car, but I don't think any of us are ready for that kind of freedom. Still, it would take some pressure off my schedule if she could manage some of the things that require transportation.

I met with Rebecca again last night. She had looked into the discrepancy with the police report. No wonder Horace Lindsey looked so upset when the knife appeared to be omitted from the report. The knife was there, on the ground beside Skipper's body. It had been marked, photographed and noted in his report to the crime scene investigation team.

Rebecca pulled out her notebook but didn't open it. "Mr. Lindsey is pretty sure Ralph Kornegay is the one who stripped the report of any mention of the knife. He said he asked him about a fingerprint report on the knife and said the chief was evasive at first, then admitted the fingerprints hadn't matched Eddie's. When Lindsey asked another question, Kornegay exploded. Lindsey figured it was just the emotional stress of losing his only son, so he backed off."

"Wow, that's...that's big."

"Mr. Lindsey is cooperating with the investigation. I'm pretty sure he doesn't want his own record tainted. He's going to do some searching in the old records, if he can get access, and see if he can turn up a report on the fingerprints. Otherwise, there is little to go on, other than the inconsistency in the reports. There may be DNA evidence on Skipper's clothing, but it's the state attorney's call whether to have them tested or not. I can put pressure on him for the story, but no guarantee he'll comply."

"Have you spoken with Barry Garrett yet?"

"Uh, briefly. He doesn't have much to say. Just told me to let him know if I uncovered anything that might be of interest to him. He gave me a copy of Miss Ora's confession, though. The story she dictated to...oh...what was her name? Claire... Clara..."

"Clara Jean Smallwood."

"That's the one."

"Yeah, I haven't read it yet," I said.

"You should," Rebecca nodded, her eyebrows raised and chin tucked down a bit. "It's an interesting read."

I frowned. I was surprised he just handed the document over to her like that.

"Mrs. Beckworth says she confronted Ralph Kornegay. She basically threatened to expose the chief's son as a rapist if he interfered in any way."

"Interfered in what?"

"Mr. Mims' confession. He intended to enter a guilty plea."

"I do remember that. My mother was heartbroken." I sighed and shook my head at the memory.

"Mrs. Beckworth told the chief if anything else happened to Mr. Mims…if he was harmed in any way, or treated badly in prison, she'd expose the whole thing, even if she went to jail herself."

Rebecca was like that. If anything got too personal, she just acted like you hadn't said a word. I was sitting there trying to think of what to say when she spoke again.

"Do you think she'd have done that?" she asked.

"Done what?"

"Gone to jail if anything else happened to Eddie." Rebecca's face was all pinched up and she was tapping the eraser end of her pencil on the outside of her leather notebook.

"I don't know, but you can certainly ask her."

"I could," she said, "but I'm asking you. I want to know what kind of woman she is, if she would let an innocent man go to jail to save *her* ass?"

I'm not sure I've thought of it that way. "My understanding was that she was simply following my mother's wishes."

Rebecca looked at me like I had two heads. "Your mother didn't know about Marcus."

"Well, yeah, but I'm referring to what set the whole thing in motion. Grace was raped. Mama didn't report it. If that hadn't happened, we wouldn't be sitting here today."

"But we are sitting here," Rebecca said reasonably. "And it's partly because Ora Lee Beckworth manipulated a lot of people in this town."

"I honestly think she meant well," I clamped my hand over my mouth.

"Maybe so. I'm not sure it turned out all that well, though."

151

"Clearly not," I said. "But how would you have handled it? I mean, knowing what you know now. Hindsight being what it is."

"I don't need hindsight," she snapped. "I know what I'd do every single time. I've always known."

I sat up straight then, and I looked her dead in the eye. "And you've always been white," I said.

"So is Ora." Rebecca sneered like she'd caught me in some kind of lie.

I willed myself calm. I paused a minute and weighed my words.

"I hope this isn't the tack you're taking on this story. My family and I do not blame Miss Ora in any way, and neither did my mother."

"Did your mother know the truth? The whole truth?"

She had me there, and she knew it.

47 – Grace

I went to see Miss Ora today. They moved her into the nursing home yesterday. I don't know what I was expecting. The way they were talking, I thought it was just a place where people went to get well, but it's all mixed in with people who just layin' there dyin' with nobody to take care of 'em. I know Miss Ora thought the same thing, 'cause when I went in her room, she looked scared half to death.

She reached for me the second I went up to her bed.

"I wanna go home," she said. Her voice still kinda cloudy, but you can understand her okay now.

"How you feelin'?" I'd brought her some roses out of the garden, tucked into a bud vase she had underneath the kitchen sink. I put those on her bedside table. "I brought some clean underwear and nightgowns from home. I figured you were tired of the hospital kind."

"Oh, Gracie," she clutched at my hand. "That's so thoughtful of you."

"I think they go'n give you a shower today. And Re'Netta's comin' by tomorrow to fix your hair. That little bit your hairdresser did done worn off."

"I don't want to stay here," she repeated.

"I know, Miss Ora. But we gotta get you well enough to come home."

"What do I have to do?"

I had to think about that for a minute. I'm not always there when the doctors come in.

"Seems like I remember them saying you had to be able to walk with a walker and stand long enough to take a shower by yourself. Oh, and get up and down the stairs, too. That's not all that much, Miss Ora. Maybe it won't take long."

She rolled her eyes. "I hate that walker."

"We can get you a better one. A snazzy one with a chair thingy you can sit in if you get tired. I saw a lady down the hallway with one."

"I'll look like a doddering old fool," she muttered under her breath.

I walked over and opened the curtains on the windows. The room looked out on a little grassy area they had decorated with little flower windmills and four or five metal stands holding bird feeders.

153

"Oh, look, Miss Ora. They have hummers here, too."

She craned her head to see the red feeder swaying in the breeze. A pair of hummingbirds swooped in, fighting each other for one of four plastic flowers.

She reached for the cord pinned to the top of her bed and raised herself up to a sitting position.

"That's better," she said. "Oh goodness, that's lovely. Not my style, but I can appreciate the effort."

"Better'n the hospital view," I said. "All you saw was the air-conditioning unit."

I stayed with her 'til they came down to take her to physical therapy, then I walked over to the church and waited for the meeting to start. I got there early enough to help set out the cookies and make the coffee. They liked when you did that, and it kinda felt good. Like I was a part of it all.

I haven't shared yet. I don't know why. I go every day. I say the prayer and I say my name, and I hold hands with people I don't even know, but I can't bring myself to tell my story. I sometimes think I can just fade away inside the group, but I been doin' this long enough to know I won't disappear. The longer I go without tellin' my story, the more I stand out and, worse, stand apart from the rest. And that ain't good. I need a sponsor, and that comes with a whole new set of troubles. I never learned to trust nobody. How you gonna trust somebody when you can't even trust the people you love the most?

48 – Patrice

Aunt Tressa went back home the day after our family meeting, but we stayed in close touch by phone. Her voice sounded remarkably like my mother's, especially when she said my name. I loved when she called to check in. It was almost like having Mama back, even though I knew better.

We settled into a summer routine that felt something close to normal. Shawn got certified in water rescue and CPR and started working three days a week at the YMCA across town. Danita picked him up on her way to work and dropped him off at Miss Ora's afterwards. Rochelle spent some of those days with Re'Netta at the shop. She put her to work answering phones and sweeping hair off the floor and paid her just enough to make it worth the effort. Occasionally, though, she asked to stay with Grace. They would often go by the public library on their way to the nursing center. Rochelle enjoyed reading aloud to Miss Ora, who still had trouble holding a book in both hands.

On the days that Shawn didn't work, both kids stayed with Grace. We got into the habit of eating supper together at Miss Ora's house on those nights. Shawn and Rochelle helped Grace take care of the house and yard. Miss Ora had a lawn service under contract for the mowing, but Grace trimmed hedges, pruned roses, and weeded the flower beds. She also started teaching Rochelle how to cook. They would bake a couple of times a week, taking cookies and cakes to share with Miss Ora and the staff at the center, or with her group at AA. I began to relax and enjoy our new normal, despite wishing Miss Ora could come home. It was nice knowing I could count on Grace for the little things.

By mid-July, I started wondering what was happening on the story Rebecca was writing. I hadn't heard from her in weeks. One night we were just finishing a supper of leftovers Grace had heated up, when the doorbell rang. I figured it was Cheryl. She often stopped by when she saw my car in the driveway.

"I'll get it," I said, rising from my chair, but Grace was already up and on her way to the door.

I followed her, expecting to join Cheryl on the porch like we always did. When she opened the door, however, there was a man standing

155

there. I guess we weren't who he was expecting either, so we all stood there in shock for a few seconds.

The man was tall and lanky, his face angular, almost sharp at the edges. He wore a polo shirt and khaki pants that fit perfectly and spoke of money. His collar bones pressed against the fabric of his shirt and his biceps stretched the band around the short sleeves. Despite all that, he looked decidedly uncomfortable. Scared almost. I couldn't think of anything to say. I just stood there staring at his face which, if I wasn't mistaken, looked vaguely familiar.

He spoke first. "I…I was looking for Mrs. Beckworth? I'm told she still lives here. Am I right? I mean…do I have the wrong house?"

"Who are *you*?" Grace demanded.

I tried to soften it some. I thought maybe he was an attorney, or possibly even a relative and I didn't want to offend. "This is Mrs. Beckworth's house, yes. She's not home right now, though. Can we help you?"

"Are you Patrice?" he asked, looking directly at me.

I nodded. "I am. Do I know you?"

"We went to school together. I'm James Hardy."

I had a vague recollection of the name, but I was still not putting things together. "What class were you in?"

"A year behind you'77. I…we…I was a friend of Skipper Kornegay's."

"Jimbo," I said.

He winced. "I go by Jim now."

I took Grace by the arm before I spoke again. She looked at me with eyes wide. She seemed frozen in place for a minute. Her mouth was open like she was about to speak, but nothing came out at all.

"Grace, honey," I spoke like I was talking to a child and, quite frankly, at that moment I think I was. "Why don't you take the kids upstairs to the game room while I talk to Mr. Hardy. I'll come get you as soon as we're through."

Grace just kept staring at the man, so I looked, too. His face, tanned by the sun with pale half-moons under his eyes, was blotched bright red across his cheeks and down his neck.

"You're Grace?" he asked, and she nodded in response.

"What is it you want?" I stepped in front of Grace then. I wasn't sure why I felt suddenly protective, but I did. With all of my being, I did.

He swallowed hard and shoved his hands in his pockets.

156

"I'm sorry, I'm just a little flustered. I came to speak to Mrs. Beckworth. I didn't realize you'd be here. I should go." He turned to leave and I stepped out of the door and onto the porch.

"Whoa, whoa, whoa," I closed the door behind me, leaving Grace standing mute in the living room. "I need to know why you're here."

He turned to face me, raising both hands with elbows tucked at his sides. "I'm not sure why, Patrice. I just knew I had to come. I...I have struggled with this for so many years and now..." He closed both hands and brought his fists together in front of his chest.

"What is this about?"

"It's about Grace. It's about what he did to her."

"You were there?" I asked, my head reeling.

"Not exactly. I was with them that day, but I didn't see it happen."

I stood looking at him for a moment. "So, I'll ask you again. *Why* are you *here*?"

"I got a call from Donnie Allred. He said there was a reporter doing a story about Skipper's murder. Said she knew about the rape and was asking questions."

"So you're covering your ass now?"

"No!" He looked horrified. "No, not at all. Exactly the opposite. Donnie asked me to cover for him. Asked me to say it never happened, or at least that they weren't there when it did. I told him I wouldn't lie for him. I can't do it anymore. I should have told the truth long ago."

"Here's the thing, Jimbo," I rubbed my eyes and tried to get my words straight. "This family has been through a lot. *Grace* has been through a lot. My sister is finally getting her life together and, quite frankly, I don't think it's healthy to ask her to forgive you for what you did or did not do. As far as I'm concerned, that's between you and God."

He stood straighter then, almost like he knew something I did not. "It's not about God's forgiveness, Patrice. I have that. It's about giving Grace the heartfelt apology she deserves. I want to tell your sister that I am sorry for what happened to her, and for not coming forward immediately. I have some contacts that might be useful, and I want to offer to help in any way I can."

"Are you an attorney?" I asked.

"No, no... I just work with them a lot."

"What is it you do, then?"

"I run a non-profit organization..." He hesitated, and I swear he looked a little sheepish. "We help battered and abused women find jobs, shelter, justice – whatever they need."

I'm not sure what I expected to hear, but it definitely wasn't that. I studied him a moment before speaking.

"Is this... was this because of Grace? What you're doing... is it because of Grace?"

"Absolutely," he said. "I got involved in a campus ministry in college and just never looked back. The thing is, it's never been enough. I've always thought about Grace specifically and felt like... I don't know... like it was the one case I'd had the opportunity to change and I'd done nothing. So, what good was what I *was* doing if I couldn't fix what I *hadn't* done? That sounds ridiculous, I know."

"No, I get it," I paused and looked hard at his face for a minute. The thing is, I believed his intentions were good. But it isn't that simple. "Listen, I need to go talk to Gracie. She's always been fragile, so I don't know if this was a good idea —"

"I know, and I'm so sorry. I had no idea y'all would be here. I was looking for Mrs. Beckworth."

"So, if you'll give me your phone number...how long will you be in town?"

"I'm in Orlando now, so it's not too far to come back. I'm going by Barry Hammond's office tomorrow morning. I have an appointment with him at 10:00."

"Okay, so if you have a business card, that's great. If Grace wants to speak to you, I'll call you and set up a time."

He pulled a card out of his pocket and handed it to me, staring at me for a second longer than was comfortable until we both looked away.

"Patrice?" I heard him, but I did not turn my head. "Is she okay?"

I felt my face go tight and my eyes filled with water. "No," I said. "No, she's really not."

"If there is anything I can do? I have resources..." His voice trailed off.

"I'll call you," I said. I went back inside and shut the door behind me

49 – Grace

I don't know how I knew, but I knew. Has to be 'cause we saw the picture in the yearbook. He looks the same and he don't look the same, but I'da never looked twice at him if we saw him on the street.

When Patrice came back inside, I was standin' in the kitchen feelin' like I had one foot nailed to the floor. She hugged me, but I couldn't seem to raise my arms to hug her back.

"How you feeling?"

"Limp as a rag doll." Lord, I sounded more like my mama every day. Or was that one of Miss Ora's sayings? I can't remember.

"Sit down, Gracie. Can I get you some tea?"

I nodded and sat at the kitchen table. Patrice looked at the dishes Shawn had stacked in the sink. Everything he do is organized. Plates stacked. Glasses side by side in a row.

"I don't know which was yours, so I'll get a new glass." She was already opening the cabinet door, so it sounded like she was talking to the dishes and not me.

"What'd he want?"

"Well..." She kinda sighed, like she was tryin' to figure out how to say whatever it was she was gonna say. "He says he was there...the day you were raped. Says he didn't actually see anything but was with the boys that day and heard about it afterwards."

"Could be true," I said. "There was four boys on bikes, but only two of 'em came back when that white-haired boy stopped."

"He's going by to talk with Mr. Hammond tomorrow. Says Donnie Allred called him about the story Rebecca's doing. I guess he's worried about being in trouble."

"How could he be in trouble if he wasn't there?"

She put two glasses of sweet tea on the table in front of me and sat down. She dragged the closest glass toward her and cupped the bottom of it with both hands.

"It's Donnie Allred who's worried. Doesn't want his name in the papers. Wanted Jimbo to say it never happened."

"Figures," I said. "What's he gonna do?"

"He says he just wants to tell the truth."

159

I just shrugged.

"There's more," Sister studied me real careful for a minute.

"What?"

"He wants to talk to you. I told him I didn't think it was a good idea. You've been through enough, and I'm worried he's just trying to make himself feel better, not you."

"Prob'ly so," I nodded. "Ain't that the way it usually goes?"

She took a sip of her tea and set it back down. "I don't know, though. I think he's sincere. I just don't know if it will do *you* any good to hear 'I'm sorry'."

"So far you the only one said that, and you didn't even know. Ya gotta kinda appreciate the offer, I guess, but it's still weird."

"He runs a program that helps women. He's been doing it since college. I think his conscience has bothered him."

I had to laugh at that. "Well, if that's what's made him keep helping people, maybe I shouldn't let him off the hook."

"It is rather ironic," Sister said. "Anyway, I told him I'd talk to you and get back to him. I personally think we need to talk to Kamilah before we do anything. I mean, if you even *want* to hear from him."

"I guess I need to think about it," I said. "I don't know whether I do or don't."

Sister looked at her watch. "It's getting late. I'm gonna get these kids home. You okay?"

"I'm fine."

I guess I wasn't all that convincing, 'cause she looked like she just wasn't sure.

"Don't worry, I won't do nothin' stupid, I promise." I stood and wiped the puddle of water from my glass with my bare hand.

Sister hugged me, then gathered up the kids and left.

I wish she knew how good somethin' stupid sounded right then.

160

50 – Patrice

I didn't tell Grace, but I was determined to be in that meeting between Jim Hardy and Barry Hammond. I called Barry at home before I went to bed and told him I'd be there, then I called Jim to let him know I'd be joining them the next morning.

He was surprised, but agreeable, and we chatted for a few minutes. Mostly about Grace – how she had not been told the truth until recently, and the impact the trauma had on her life.

"I can't imagine what it was like for Grace, I mean…women almost always face denial from the perpetrator. Denial, minimalization, gaslighting. But to have her own mother deny it when she knew the truth, that's tough. On the other hand, most rapes *aren't* reported for the same reason…fear. It's the reason I didn't come forward. I was terrified."

"I guess what I'm wondering," I said after an awkward pause, "is why now? Would you have come forward if there wasn't a story being written? Feels like damage control to me."

"I'm sure it looks that way, but I've told this story many times in my work. How I was a teenager and knew about a rape I didn't report. How frightened I was, and how the guilt has haunted me over the years. For most of my colleagues, this will not come as a surprise. The only difference now is there are names and faces to go along with the story. Was it spurred by the report? Yes. And yet, I'm here. And I'm offering an apology and any help I can provide Grace to get through this. I believe in my program. I've seen the results. And I owe Grace every single thing at my disposal. This offer is good no matter what happens. I give you my word."

It was a generous offer, and yet, something about it bothered me. "I'll see you in the morning." I hung before he had a chance to respond.

***

I arrived a half hour early and had a cup of coffee with Barry. He gave me little in the way of information about the case.

161

"We're investigating," he said. "That's all you need to know right now. I'm actually glad this guy...what's his name?"

"James Hardy. Jimbo. I guess he goes by Jim now."

"Jim, that's it." Barry tugged on his desk drawer and rummaged through it until he found a packet of sweetener. He flipped it onto the desk beside his coffee mug but didn't open it. "What do you know about him?"

"Not much. I went to school with him, but we weren't friends. He seems sincere, says all the right things, but something's off. I can't put my finger on it."

"Well, I'm glad he's coming by. I didn't feel like his buddy was forthcoming on his role, so I'm anxious to hear his story."

"Which buddy?"

"Allred, I think it was. I'm not sure exactly. I've got someone else on the case, so all this is secondhand."

I'm not sure why, but a lightbulb clicked on in my head.

"Did you..." I hesitated because I frankly didn't want to make him mad. But, no, I was sure I was right. "Who'd you say you assigned the case to?"

His head sort of snapped up and he looked confused for a second. "I don't think I said. I'll have to get back to you on that."

I frowned at him. We were adversaries in a lot of things, but we were, at the very least, *friends* outside of work.

"Barry..."

"What?" He picked up the pink packet, tore off the top and sprinkled white powder into his coffee cup.

"Did you give this to Rebecca Yager?"

I'd seen this before. It's called the court of public opinion. A prosecutor up for re-election will send a story to the newspaper to gauge the public's reaction before deciding how to proceed. Personally, I think it's a bit cowardly, and I was more than a little surprised he would go this route. On the other hand, if it went our way, it might not be a bad thing.

He took a sip from his cup and I could see him trying to keep a straight face.

"Okay, okay...busted. But can you blame me? I mean, hell, I don't even know who there would be to charge with anything. The rapist is dead. The old man is dead. The boy's killer is dead. What am I gonna do, put an old lady in jail for destroying evidence? Accessory after the fact? What? I can't see it. But I can't ignore it, either."

I just shook my head. He had a point.

Jim arrived ten minutes later. His story was brief. He said Donnie Allred and Allen Madison stopped by his house later that day and told him what they saw.

"What was their demeanor when they told you?" I asked.

Jim looked embarrassed. "I don't think you want to know."

"I wouldn't be here if I didn't want to know," I said.

"Allen was kind of quiet about it, but Donnie thought it was funny."

Barry winced and rocked back in his chair.

"Did you think it was funny?" I pressed.

Jim took a deep breath. He didn't want to answer the question. I've seen that look before.

"I laughed, but I didn't think it was funny. I never thought it was funny."

The room got deadly quiet. I didn't trust myself to speak.

"So this was in, what, September?" Barry finally broke the silence.

"I think so, yeah."

"And you were still hanging around with them at Halloween?" Barry had clearly done his homework.

"Not as much," Jim said. "But, yes, we stopped by Miss Ora's house to see if we could score some Halloween candy. She was acting weird though. She used to teach us in Sunday School, so we all knew her well. Seemed like she knew what happened, so I wanted to leave. Skipper was challenging her, though. I'll never forget it. That's why I came to see her yesterday. I wanted to ask her how she knew."

Barry leaned forward then. "Yeah, she knew all right. Listen, I'd like to get a deposition from you, if that's okay. We can set it up for later this week. It's no big deal, but I'd like to get these stories on the record before the information is released to the public. I just don't see anything I can prosecute at this time. I would caution you, however, to speak to your attorney before you do anything."

Jimbo just shook his head. "I can do it today. I've already discussed this with several attorneys who think I'm nuts, but I don't care. I want it off my conscience."

"Suit yourself," Barry said, then punched a button on his phone and summoned his legal assistant. When she answered he said, "Have we got time for a deposition either this morning or after lunch? I'll need you in on it, but I'll be deposing the witness. James Hardy."

The phone crackled a little and she answered, "I can do 2:15 if that works for you."

"Perfect," Barry said and ended the call.

Jim and I left together and headed for our cars.

"Can I take you to lunch?" he asked.

"Ah, sure," I said, feeling awkward at best, and disloyal at worst. "I was going to stop by to see Miss Ora first. You can follow me if you like."

51 – Grace

I was helping Miss Ora into her robe when Patrice came in. She looked surprised to see me, even though I told her I visit Miss Ora every day. She told me she'd met with Jimbo Hardy that morning and he wanted to talk to both of us if that was okay.

To tell the truth, I'm not all that excited about talkin' to any of them boys. Ain't nothin' they can say to change anything. But it's hard to blame this one. He wasn't even there when it happened. And Miss Ora wanted to see him, so Sister brought him to the room. I couldn't tell who was more nervous, him or Miss Ora. I didn't feel nervous at all, just irritated.

I gotta say, though, the man is smooth. Whether he means what he's sayin' or not, you believe him. But maybe he's just sayin' all the right things 'cause he knows what he's talkin' about.

Miss Ora remembered him pretty good. He told her he was sorry they'd been such jerks to her that Halloween night. "It just seemed like you knew something about Skipper, and I was embarrassed."

Miss Ora nodded. "I knew."

"I wish I'd done everything different. I just want you to know that I'm sorry, Grace. I'm so sorry this happened to you. I was raised in a good home, by *good* parents, and I should have done better. I've spent my adult life trying to atone for this, to pay it forward and help other women who've suffered the way you did. If there is anything I can do…anything…I will do it. All you have to do is ask."

It felt weird watching a grown man's eyes fill with tears. That's somethin' I ain't never seen before. I almost felt sorry for him. But then, what do you say?

All I could think to say was, "Thank you." That was the best I could do. I stood there, awkward as hell, wishin' he would just leave.

Miss Ora broke the silence. "So were you there when it happened? I'm confused about that."

"Oh, no, no…we all rode through together, but I was in a hurry to get home, so I was ahead of them. We were halfway through town when Allen yelled at me to hold up and wait for Skipper. We stopped and waited for a minute, and he still didn't show up, so they decided to go back. I wish I'd gone with them. I have to believe I'd have stopped him. But it was Wednesday, and I was late for church. Allen told me later..."

He got really choked up then and stopped talking.

"It's okay," I told him, and I meant it. It's done and over with. Ain't no use cryin' now.

"I'm so sorry, Grace. Please forgive me."

I took a deep breath and let it out. All I could think was, if I forgive him, he'll leave and I can just go on. I was about to speak when I noticed Patrice studyin' the man with her lawyer face. I knew she was fixin' to nail him on something. I've seen that look too many times before.

"Why didn't you tell?"

He looked surprised by the question. "I...I was terrified."

"Of whom?" Patrice frowned.

"Well...of Skipper and his daddy, I guess. Then, the longer I went without telling, the harder it was. Especially when I saw you at school..."

"Wait..." Sister interrupted him. "You knew who she was?"

"Yeah, Allen recognized her. He said she was your little sister, which made it even worse. The guilt was awful. I never forgot, though, and I've spent my whole life trying to make amends for not stepping up. That's why I started Grace Ministries right out of college. I—"

I gripped the railing on Miss Ora's bed and leaned toward him. "You used my *name*?"

"No, I...well, kind of, I mean..." He backed up against the door with his hands spread wide. "It was more like a double entendre. It's a faith-based ministry and it just...it just seemed right."

"It's my *name*." I felt my bottom lip push forward like I was a child and I clenched my lips together trying not to lose it. "*My* name. Mine."

I was shaking so bad, I had to sit down. I put my head in my hands and started rocking back and forth.

"I think you need to leave." Miss Ora's voice sounded shaky, too.

"I'm sorry. I'm really sorry," I heard him say, but it sounded like he was in a tunnel.

I heard the door open and close and the room got quiet. When I opened my eyes, it was just me and Miss Ora in the room.

52 – Patrice

I followed Jim Hardy to the parking lot. He was pale and kept mopping his forehead with a white handkerchief.

"You should have warned me about the name," I said.

"I didn't think of it. I just didn't. It has been this name the entire time."

It took only seconds for the enormity, the gravity of this meeting, the intentions of this man, to settle on me. It is an oppressive weight I've felt all my life, and it never gets any easier to bear.

"Did you ever stop to consider that you built an entire career on *her* story? A story you have told over and over for your own benefit and never *once* for hers? You had the least to lose, Jimbo. Throughout all of this, you were the one person who had nothing to fear."

"I was a kid. I made a mistake."

"And you made another one coming here today."

"I came to apologize."

"No, you came for forgiveness. You came for redemption. Like she owes you or something. But what did you risk? Nothing. Nothing at all. You rode in on your big *white* horse like you're some kind of hero. Well, don't kid yourself. You're not. Everything you've done – every single thing – is to make yourself feel better. It's got nothing to *do* with how Grace feels."

"I don't want that to be true." I could see tears welling up in his eyes and his voice grew strained and hoarse. "I wanted her to know I was sorry."

"Right. I get that. You wanted her to know you were sorry so *you* would feel better. Even worse, you think she's the one who needs pity. Wrong. Wrong, Jimbo. You're the one. *You* are the one."

I watched him walk toward his car, a Mercedes coupe that looked out of place in the parking lot of a nursing home. He opened the door, then looked back at me like he wanted to say something. I waited, but he did not speak. He slid into the driver's seat and disappeared behind the tinted window.

I turned to go back inside and saw Grace standing silently by the door. She looked small, wounded, lost. I reached her in four steps and folded her into my arms.

"I'm sorry, Grace. I should have known better than to bring him."

"I need help, Sister."

"I know you do. I know."

***

I called Kamilah on the way home. She said she would find out which centers had a bed available and meet us at Miss Ora's house. Grace and I were sitting on the porch when she arrived. I went inside to pack Grace's clothes and give them time to talk. I didn't need to stop to think what I'd do with Rochelle and Shawn. I had a support system in place.

I called Miss Ora at the nursing center and told her what was happening. She said she'd be fine at the center as long as Grace was gone. I told her I'd work on getting a home healthcare nurse if she was ready sooner, but she was adamant.

"If Grace can stay in rehab, so can I," she said. "And I'll stay as long as it takes her to get well. It's the least I can do."

"That's fine, but you just let me know when you're ready, and we'll make it happen."

"I'll be ready when Gracie's ready," Miss Ora's voice shook with emotion. "She is coming home, isn't she?"

"Yes, ma'am," I said. "She is definitely coming home."

53 – Grace

I don't know how I knew it was time. I was standing there in the room with Miss Ora thinkin', if something doesn't change *today*, I'm gonna use. It's too much. It hurts *too* much. I thought if I just had someone to take care of, the hurt would go away. I wanted the kids to be enough to make me forget. But I have it backwards. I gotta deal with the pain or I'm never gonna be enough for them. I gotta take care of me before I can take care of anybody else.

When we got home, I sat on the porch with Sister and waited for Kamilah to get there. She's gonna take me to the rehab center in Gainesville. Sister asked me if I wanted to wait 'til tomorrow...if I wanted to say goodbye to my babies.

I said, "If I wait, I won't go."

She just nodded and squeezed my hand.

"I'm gonna miss this porch."

She laughed. "Next time you see it, Miss Ora will be sitting out here."

"I sure hope so."

"And Shawn will have his learner's permit."

"Lord help," I said.

54 – Patrice

Three weeks after Grace signed herself into the recovery center, Rebecca Yager-Mills' article came out in the Mayville Tribune. Barry Hammond called me two days later and asked me to stop by to discuss the case.

When his assistant ushered me into his office, he greeted me warmly, seated me in one of the chairs in front of his desk, then sat beside me in the other.

"You've read the article, I assume?" He had the newspaper in his hand, folded in half and then again to reveal just the half page article bearing the headline *Local Woman Seeks Justice for The Pecan Man*.

"Oh, yeah, I read it."

"What'd you think?"

"Pretty impressive reporting. She's an amazing storyteller," I said.

"She's good. I won't be surprised if she starts getting offers from the big guns."

I laughed. "You think it's that good?"

"I do. Part human interest and part exposé...it has all the right elements. I'm still sweating it a little though. Could be a career breaker for me."

"So that's why you went the media route?"

"Hey, it's an election year. One wrong move and I'd be out of a job. I wasn't all that happy when you laid it in my lap. Too complicated. Too personal. Too many variables."

"Trust me, I get it. I felt the same way when Miss Ora dumped it on me."

"How's she doing, by the way. I heard she'd had a stroke."

"She's coming along. She'll actually be ready to come home in the next few weeks, but she has decided she's staying in the nursing center until Grace comes home."

"Where'd Grace go?"

Where'd Grace go, indeed. I couldn't help smiling. I thought of my sister's face as she said goodbye and climbed into Kamilah's SUV. I have never seen her so determined, so confident, so ready to be well.

"She checked herself into rehab," I said.

Barry leaned forward and placed a hand on my shoulder.

"Oh, Patrice, that is wonderful news."

"It is, isn't it?"

"Honestly, it couldn't have happened at a better time. Just as well she's out of town until this blows over."

"How bad do you think it's going to be?" I hadn't heard much myself, but that wasn't unusual. I don't watch much television, and rarely the local news at all. Truth be told, I was lying low.

"I'm feeling pretty good about it, actually. Kornegay's family isn't too happy. Our city police are a little on edge. Horace Lindsey is catching some heat, but he says he doesn't care. It was his report that was falsified, his signature forged, and his reputation on the line. He says he understands why the chief did it, but he doesn't appreciate having his own actions brought into question. If it goes to court, he's willing to testify accordingly."

I winced. I didn't like the sound of that. "I was sure hoping it wouldn't get that far."

"It won't. I've had several ASA's look at it, too. We all believe the same thing. Once we exclude anything beyond the statute of limitations, we're left with basically nothing. We could commission an investigation by internal affairs, but there is no indication this was a systemic problem in Kornegay's force. If it had been, we'd have seen evidence of it long before this."

"I don't know," I said, "this could prompt a few people to cry foul on their own cases. I'm going to bet there will be more than one defense attorney digging through their case files."

"No doubt about it, but we'll cross those bridges when we get to them. For now, I am going to decline to press charges in this case."

"Whatever happened with Skipper's friends?"

"Ha!" Barry shifted in his chair. "Did I not tell you about that?"

"I haven't spoken to you since the day of Jim Hardy's deposition."

"Yeah, that was the one that threw me. He was all gung-ho to tell his story before you left, but he never showed for the deposition. We tried to call him several times, left messages on his phone, but he never returned our calls. A week later, we got a letter from his attorney saying we'd need to direct further inquiry to their office."

I just sat there a minute, stunned and silent.

"Wow," I said finally. "Just wow."

"I wondered what you said to piss him off."

"I just told him I thought this was all for his own benefit and not Grace's."

"And he proved you right, didn't he?"

"Yeah, he did," I said. "How about the other two?"

"Donnie Allred was pretty clear he had no intentions of cooperating. He said if we charged him, he'd get an attorney. Otherwise he wanted to be left alone. The other guy, Allen something...he said he'd testify if it went to court. So, you know, that was it for me. I got nothing. I'm not going to waste time and money on a case that has nowhere to go."

"What about Miss Ora?" I thought I knew the answer, but I wanted to hear it from him.

"I would have my ass handed to me on a platter if I charged an old woman in a nursing home for anything. The statutes are out on everything anyway, thank God."

My relief was immediate and visceral. I almost cried, but I willed myself to be calm and poised, just like I'd been trained to do. Still, my hands shook as I reached for my briefcase on the floor between our chairs.

"Where you going?" Barry asked.

The question confused me.

"Uh, back to my office?" I wasn't sure why I answered with a question, so I added, "Why?"

"I wondered what you would say if I asked you to lunch. A little celebration of sorts."

"Oh, gosh...I would say...I would say I have to think about it."

He wrinkled up his face and raised himself out of his chair. He offered me his hand so I stood, too.

"Okay, I've got a few minutes. Think about it... starting... *now*." He walked around his desk, took his suit coat off the coat rack and put it on.

I just shook my head and laughed.

"Have you thought about it yet?" He grinned like the joke was on me.

"Are you seriously flirting with me?"

"That depends on whether it's working or not."

The truth is, the thought of going to lunch with Barry Hammond was pretty intriguing. As friends, not so unusual. We'd socialized in groups plenty of times. But this felt different, caught me off guard. I'm not used to being off guard. I opened my mouth to speak, but nothing really came out.

"So that's a no?"

I was surprised at how disappointed he looked.

"I don't think so."

"You don't think you'll go to lunch with me? Or you don't think it's a no?"

"I don't think it's a no," I said.

The man actually clapped his hands together. "Whoop! I'm halfway there."

"Don't get too excited now. It's just lunch." I turned and started for the door and he caught up with me.

"Well, duh, it was always just lunch. You don't have to worry until I ask you to dinner."

"Good to know," I said, which made him laugh out loud.

Don't overthink this, Patrice, I said to myself as he opened the passenger door and waited for me to settle in.

And as he walked around the back of the car, I heard my mother's voice, as clear in my head as if she were sitting there with me, *Everything go'n be all right, baby girl. Everything go'n be fine.*

Epilogue
Ora Lee Beckworth

"Mama? Mama! Can you come help me?" Rochelle's voice carried down the hallway where I was trying to take a nap. I'm back on my feet now, but I don't venture up the stairs much these days.

Grace moved me into Walter's old room when we got out of rehab. I nearly drove her crazy trying to hang onto things that just needed to go. I sat in his mother's old gooseneck chair in the corner and watched as she pulled out old ties – *I bought that one for his mother's funeral, and the red striped one for a Fourth of July celebration downtown* – and sorted through cufflinks and watches – *Patty at the jewelry store helped me pick those out* – and a variety of suits ranging from gray to black and nothing in between. I'd never missed my husband as I did when I gathered his belongings and donated them to Goodwill. I think I always felt like he was just away on business and any minute would walk back in the door. In my own way, it was grief that made me hold on to the physical things and push down the emotional ones. As always, I just put one foot in front of the other and did what needed to be done.

"Just a minute, Rochelle, I'm busy," Grace yelled back from upstairs. But I heard her chair roll across the floor and her sure footsteps on the stairs as she went to her daughter in the kitchen.

I inched out of my bed and slid my feet into the soft slippers I kept at the side of my bed. I used to dress every single day, but I've decided I'm old enough to stay in a housedress all day if I want to. And today I wanted to.

I shuffled down the hallway and into the kitchen. Rochelle was baking cookies for a class party the next day. I secretly hoped she'd save me one or two, but I didn't ask.

"Smells good in here," I said.

"Did we wake you up?" Grace leaned over and kissed me on the cheek.

"No," I lied. "I was just resting my eyes."

"You go on out to the porch now," she said. "I'll bring you a cup of coffee and a cookie when they're done."

"Spoiling me again," I crooned on the way to the porch.

It was a glorious late September afternoon, the slightest hint of fall in the air. Dovey already had her mailbox decorated with fake sunflowers and straw, and a metal scarecrow stuck in the ground at its base. It has been almost a year since Grace and I came home, and I marvel at every single day I wake up and I am still here. I count my progress by how many mailbox changes I get to see and sometimes, if I'm feeling particularly morbid, I wonder which will be my last.

Dovey still stops by every now and then, and her daughter is here even more often. We buried the hatchet when the newspaper article came out, though I first thought I'd have to bury it in her behind. You'd think she'd be scared of waving a newspaper in my face, but she hustled right over to the nursing home the day it came out.

She peeked her head through the crack in the door with the newspaper clutched in her hand. "Is it true? Is all of this true?"

"Lord, what took you so long, Dovey?" I waved her inside. I'd already had phone calls from women who hadn't called on me in years. They all knew where to find me, prayer chains being so informative and all, so I was expecting Dovey.

"Funny, Ora *Lee*." She emphasized my first name to remind me she'd long since stopped deferring to my age.

"Oh, come on, Dovey. I'm old and I'm tired. I don't have any fight left."

"I don't wanna fight you, Ora Lee. I just want to know how much of this is true. I mean, not that it's any of my business..."

"Truer words have not been spoken." She clammed up then and I took pity on her. "Help me out of this bed, would you? Let's sit over there by the window so we can visit, and I'll tell you all about it."

That's the thing with Southern women. We just need to be needed. Asking for help is almost the same as an apology sometimes. She put down her newspaper and made a fuss over getting me up and over to the recliner.

"You want your water over there, too?" She picked up my Styrofoam cup and brought it to me without waiting for an answer. Then she pushed the button on my bed and asked for "a ginger ale for Miss Ora," which, of course, was not for me at all.

When she finally settled into the hard plastic chair across from me, I thanked her and then said, "It's all true, Dovey. Every word of it."

Lord knows I wish she would think before she speaks, but the first words out of her mouth were, "Oh, Ora, you must be mortified!"

I just chuckled. "Can't even show my face in town. Whatever will I do?"

"You really don't care what people will say?"

"I really do *not*."

She looked bewildered for a moment, but then there was this little wave of, I guess you'd call it relief, that flitted across her face. Like the idea that you could just decide not to worry what people thought was absolutely liberating.

After that, we had a nice long conversation and cleared the air. I can't say we've been best buddies ever since, but we get along just fine.

When I finally did make it home four months later, it was to a spotless house and a yard that looked like no one had ever been gone. Dovey left me a note with a list of all the things I "wouldn't need to worry about."

Of course, when I tried to thank her for it, she just said, "Well, I couldn't just sit by and watch the neighborhood go to pot." But that's just Dovey for you. She means well.

Rebecca Yager-Mills won several awards for her series on racism in the judicial system. Eddie's story was one of several and became an exposé on privilege and abuse of power. She did not go easy on me in the article. Quite frankly, I'd have questioned her journalistic integrity if she had. I know what I did wrong. I live with it every day.

We have filed for a posthumous pardon for Eddie, but we have resigned ourselves that it may never happen. Without the knife, there is little evidence to go on other than my word which is understandably in question. It's ironic that I spent most of my life doing everything I believed to be right and honest but will likely be remembered for my deceit. I've heard it said that when we know better, we do better. My experience is, when we learn different, we do different. Better is a matter of perspective.

Patrice still works for the public defender's office, but she travels a bit now. She does pro bono work for the Innocence Project of Florida and the Southern Poverty Law Center. The Bible says to sow your seed in fertile ground. I don't regret a penny of my investment.

She and Kamilah and Cheryl Kincaid have big plans for my house once I'm gone. Kamilah stops by every now and then just to say hello. Every time I open the door and see her standing there I just grin and say, "I'm not dead yet!" She just laughs and laughs.

176

Grace is working on her G.E.D. right now and plans on going to college once Shawn and Rochelle are gone. I told her she could go now, but she says she's already missed enough of her kids' lives and doesn't want to miss a minute more. She's been clean and sober since before she went to the rehab center. She told me once they said relapse was part of recovery and she was dead set on proving them wrong.

I have never been prouder of anyone in my life.

Note from the Author

When I wrote The Pecan Man, I had no intentions of writing a sequel, but as many of you have told me, the characters took on a life of their own and the story didn't seem to be over. I've often been asked if Grace was going to be all right, and I'd always answer, "I don't know." The thing is, my experience has been with addicts who did not get better, who never even admitted they had a problem. I knew addiction, not recovery.

During the years I avoided writing the sequel, I lost my sister Petey and her youngest daughter Jamey Lea in the opioid crisis gripping our country. Four months after my sister passed away, my mother died of what we can only believe was a broken heart. She just stopped living.

So to say this book was difficult to write is just a huge understatement. I tried to educate myself a little by going to Al-Anon, a twelve-step program for families of addicts and alcoholics. I also consulted books on addiction and recovery, just to get an idea of the professional side of the recovery process. Debra Jay's It Takes a Family, and Debra and Jeff Jay's Love First were instrumental in helping me sort out my original idea to have the entire family participate in therapy with Grace. Turns out it really is a thing!

That being said, this novel is a work of fiction. It is not intended in any way to be instructive or a substitute for professional help. I would just like to take this opportunity to encourage readers to seek the services of a healthcare professional if you have a loved one who is an addict. I know firsthand how families are torn apart by the destructive nature of this disease. Our once very close family became fragmented and distant. Those of us left are doing our best to heal and love each other.

I couldn't help thinking as I did my research, how I wish our family had known where to turn in those years when all of us were enablers in our own way. All I know is, if love was enough, my mother could have healed them. But love without a plan is a recipe for heartbreak. It was too much for all of us individually. And we didn't know how to manage it as a family.

Thank you all for your support. Readers have been instrumental in propelling The Pecan Man into a best-selling Amazon novel. I will always be grateful.

For more information, please follow me on my Facebook pages, *Obstinate Daughters Press, Cassie Dandridge Selleck* and *The Pecan Man,* or visit my website and blog.

www.CassieDandridgeSelleck.com
www.thepecanman.wordpress.com

Writers, please visit us at www.obstinatedaughters.com and see what we have available to help you publish your work.

Made in the USA
San Bernardino, CA
20 February 2019